Wolf, No Wolf

ALSO BY PETER BOWEN

Specimen Song

Coyote Wind

Imperial Kelly

Kelly Blue

Yellowstone Kelly

WOLF, NO WOLF

⚜

A GABRIEL DU PRÉ MYSTERY

Peter Bowen

St. Martin's Press
New York

Design by Sara Stemen

Library of Congress Cataloging-in-Publication Data

Bowen, Peter, 1945–
    Wolf, no wolf: a Gabriel Du Pré mystery / by
    Peter Bowen.—1st ed.
        p.   cm.
     ISBN 0–312–14078–9
     1. Montana—Fiction.   I. Title
    PS3552.0866W65   1996
    813'.54—dc20   95–44420

10 9 8 7 6 5 4 3 2

For Alston

Wolf, No Wolf

✦ C H A P T E R 1 ✦

Du Pré fiddled in the Toussaint Bar. The place was packed. Some of Madelaine's relatives had come down from Canada to visit. It was fall and the bird hunters had come, to shoot partridges and grouse on the High Plains.

The bird hunters were pretty OK. The big game hunters were pigs, mostly. The bird hunters were outdoors people; they loved it and knew it, or wanted to. The big game hunters wanted to shoot something big, often someone's cows.

Bart had bought a couple thousand dollars' worth of liquor and several kegs of beer and there was a lot of food people had brought. Everything was free.

Kids ran in and out. The older ones could have beers. Bart was tending bar. Old Booger Tom sat on one of the high stools, cane leaned up against the front of the bar.

"You do that pretty good for someone the booze damn near killed," said Booger Tom. "I know folks won't be in the same room with the stuff."

"Find Jesus," said Bart. "It's not too late to change your life."

He went down to the far end of the bar and took orders. Susan Klein, who owned the saloon, was washing glasses at a great pace.

One of Madelaine's relatives was playing the accordion, another an electric guitar. They were very good.

Du Pré finished. He was wet with sweat. The place was

1

hot and damp and smoky, so smoky it was hard to see across the room. The room wasn't all that big, either.

Madelaine got up from her seat, her pretty face flushed from drinking the sweet pink wine she loved. She threw her arms around Du Pré and she kissed him for a long time.

"Du Pré," she said, "you make me ver' happy, you play those good songs."

Du Pré took a glass of whiskey passed hand over hand from the bar.

"Pretty good," said Du Pré, looking at the whiskey.

"What is pretty good?" said Madelaine.

"Only two people they drink a little from it, on the long journey from the bar to me."

"They love you, Du Pré," said Madelaine. She laughed. She was wearing a red, gold, green, and blue vest she had beaded herself. It had taken four years to do; the beads were tiny and she had four children.

Someday this fine woman marry me, thought Du Pré, soon as that damn Catholic church, it tell her OK, your missing husband is dead now so you can quit sinning, fornicating with Du Pré.

"Du Pré!" It was the big clumsy priest, Father Van Den Heuvel. Du Pré liked him. When Madelaine badgered Du Pré into going to confession Du Pré would confess to living in sin with Madelaine Placquemines. The priest would say, Good, I am happy for you, five Hail Marys, say them, the words are pretty.

"Such fine music!"

Father Van Den Heuvel could hear and he had a beautiful singing voice, but he was so uncoordinated he often knocked himself out slamming his head in car doors.

"Play 'The Big Rapids,' " said Father Van Den Heuvel.

"OK," said Du Pré. "I will get you some food, here."

"I can . . ."

"No," said Du Pré. "You spill a plate, fine, you knock

2

the whole damn table over, people go hungry. I go get it.''

Du Pré snaked his way through the crowd, got to the food table, piled a big plate full of meat and potato salad and fry bread and cole slaw. He carried it back.

"You sit down," said Du Pré, "then I give it to you."

The priest sat at Madelaine's table. She stood by the chair so he wouldn't go over getting into it.

Du Pré stood, sipping his whiskey.

The out-of-state bird hunters were easy to spot—very expensive hunting clothes, usually British; they smelled of dogs and gunpowder and sage. Some of the ranchers leased their land for hunting. The bird hunters who lived in Montana weren't bitter yet, but they would be when the hunting lands were all closed to them and given over to flatlanders, who could afford large fees.

"Some good party, eh?" said Du Pré to Madelaine.

She nodded. More people were coming in. Two couples from the west side of the Wolf Mountains. Stemples and Rosses. Du Pré had inspected their cattle many times, checking the brands, never any problem. Du Pré waved to them. The two couples snaked their way through the crowd and up to him.

"Du Pré!" said Bill Stemple. He held out his hand. Du Pré shook it and nodded and smiled at the others.

"We got a problem," said Stemple.

"Ah?" said Du Pré.

"Couple days ago a couple came to the house and asked if they could hunt. They seemed OK. Californians, but what the hell. We said sure. Didn't get the license numbers, of course. And then I was out driving to check my water tanks and I found some cut fences. Cattle out all over the place."

"Jesus," said Du Pré.

"Well, you don't like to think bad of folks 'less you know it," said Bill Stemple, "and it got worse. A lot of cows had been shot, with a twenty-two. I got a vet out there and it looks like I'll lose about twenty. Some were already down and dead. I have stock up in the mountains still, too, sent a couple hands, bring them down early, I'll hay 'em out."

"Got us, too," said Sally Ross. "Same story, we lost seventeen for sure and might lose that many more."

Twenty thousand dollars maybe, thought Du Pré, each. Depends. When they count it up, all, I bet twenty thousand.

"OK," said Du Pré, "I will get my coat and we will go."

"Oh, tomorrow," said Sally Ross. "They're gone, whoever they were—they didn't come to our place."

"What they look like?" said Du Pré.

"Twenties, city people, new hunting clothes. Had a springer in the back, so I thought they were all right. Those are good dogs."

"You talk to Benny?"

"Why we came," said Sally Ross. "His office said he was here." Benny Klein, the Sheriff, and his wife Susan owned the bar. Not much happened in the county that they didn't know about, and damn soon at that.

"I have not seen him," said Du Pré. "You maybe ask Susan."

The guitar player was tuning. Du Pré went back up to the little stage in the corner and he twisted the pegs on his fiddle till the tones held right.

Some shit, he thought, we got people steal cattle. Had a crazy person once poisoning people's dogs. Cattle are very valuable. Cut the fences, run them into a truck. Plenty of small places butcher them out and make real good profit. Ninety-nine percent.

Well, Du Pré thought, plenty big fight over the West, now. These new people, they sure don't care for anything that was here, or anyone. Place like this too good to last.

Well, it is worse out in the west part of the state. Not so many people here, good.

Something is changing.

Du Pré fiddled for another hour, long songs, backup, no breaks. His fingers began to hurt and then they went numb and then his hand began to cramp. He hadn't been looking out at the crowd.

The people were all silent and staring at him. Then they began to clap and hoot and whistle. It went on for several minutes.

Me, Du Pré thought, I always play fiddle better, I am angry or want to fuck or I am happy drunk, lose myself in this music. This time I am mad.

Why these people come here? Do I go to their house, mess it up? Why?

Benny Klein came in, stood, spotted Du Pré. He waved to him, come over. Du Pré put his fiddle in the case and he took it to Madelaine and then he wound through the crowd to Benny. Benny put a hand on Du Pré's shoulder and pulled him outside.

"They told you?" said Benny.

"Yah," said Du Pré. "Pretty strange, lot of money. You know what it is about?"

"Oh," said Benny, "it gets worse. There was more over north and east. But they did find, the next county over, some of that get-the-cattle-off-the-public-lands crap."

"Yah," said Du Pré, "I thought so."

Du Pré had read an article which said all the ranchers and their cattle and their families and towns should be removed from eastern Montana and the western Dakotas. Then those tens of thousands of square miles could be a big park for buffalo and wolves, so that tourists could play in it. So some of those people who wanted that could not wait; they killed the ranchers' cattle, to try to drive the ranchers away. Hah.

"Du Pré," said Benny, "I got a real bad feeling. These idiots are here, and they know they're right. They don't care about the people here. They just want what they want. They don't seem to much care how they get it."

Du Pré nodded.

"They don't know where they are," said Benny. "They drive through this country, and they think there ain't anyone in it. If their car breaks down, though, someone's there in what, fifteen minutes?"

Du Pré nodded.

"What bothers me is that no one saw them," said Benny.

Du Pré looked at Benny for a long moment.

Benny rolled a smoke. He looked very troubled.

"I make you this bet," said Du Pré. "I say there are maybe two of them."

Benny nodded.

"I say that you get some missing-persons reports, pretty soon."

Benny nodded.

"They are dead," said Du Pré. "We just have not found them."

Benny looked up.

"I won't bet you," he said. "'Cause I know you're right."

✣ CHAPTER 2 ✣

Du Pré waited for Taylor Martin to come in his helicopter at ten A.M.

"The air's better then," Martin had said. "It kinda jumps around first few hours of light."

Du Pré rolled a cigarette and lit it and he unbuttoned his leather jacket.

Them Martins, they got a ranch so damn big takes three helicopters to round up the cattle, Du Pré thought. That is a lot more ranch and cattle than I could stand.

He heard the thwock of the rotor blades. Taylor Martin and his machine rose up out of a canyon five miles away and shot along ten feet above the ground. The man flew like a cowboy rides, fast, loose, and perfectly. He set the little machine down and Du Pré ran for it through a stinging storm of dust and chaff. Du Pré ducked in and fumbled with the seat belt. Martin was pulling up before Du Pré had swung his legs completely in.

Martin set the helicopter northwest in a climb. The two men stared out at the land below, riven with coulees, the rock outcrops dark with junipers. Looking for something that shouldn't be where it was.

"The scablands?" yelled Martin.

"Start there," Du Pré yelled back.

Martin quartered back and forth. Du Pré looked off toward the ridges that led to the foothills of the Wolf Mountains, glancing at the clusters of ranch buildings, looking for a truck or car, the flash of sun on glass. Where a truck or car shouldn't have a reason to be.

The helicopter vibrated. Du Pré hated it.

This damn thing fly apart all at once, three bolts and some tinfoil. There I'll be. Hail Mary. Splat.

A coyote scooted across a meadow, ducked into the shadows of a rocky slit in the earth. Du Pré glanced down at the two automatic shotguns mounted on the struts. Martin strafed coyotes with them.

"Down there!" yelled Taylor Martin. The helicopter's noise nearly drowned his voice. Du Pré leaned out and looked. A tan four-wheel-drive Land Rover was crumpled down in the bottom of a narrow slit in the earth lined with rock. Magpies and ravens covered the bushes around the wreck, were hopping in and out of the broken windows.

Out on the scablands, Du Pré thought, shoot them, toss them in the back, drive the car over the slide there. Didn't even bother to burn it. Attract attention, anyway.

The helicopter sheared away and headed back. Martin was talking into the microphone. Du Pré could see Benny Klein's car roaring up the dirt road several miles away. He leaned over to the pilot's ear and shouted for him to land Du Pré in front of Benny.

He is a nice man, don't like dead bodies, eyes pecked out already by them damn magpies. Can't even shoot them anymore, they are protected.

Taylor Martin set the helicopter down on the road and Du Pré hopped out and the chopper took off. Du Pré rolled a smoke and he lit it and waited. Benny's car roared up, no lights flashing. Not much traffic here, for sure.

Du Pré moved to the side of the road. Benny slowed and stopped and Du Pré got in.

"I don't need this," said Benny. "You were right."

"We get there," said Du Pré, "I go look, tell you when to call the coroner."

"Governor's already asked for the FBI," said Benny. "I hope none of them get killed. This is real bad, Gabriel, real bad. I knew it would happen, too. I'm going to resign."

Du Pré nodded.

Benny, he never was made for that job, he thought, this will end with arresting our friends and neighbors.

But I will probably do it. Death, it is a pretty harsh sentence for being young fools.

"Up there," said Du Pré. He pointed to a rutted track.

Benny's cruiser bumped along the pounded earth. He

had to move slowly and steer around rocks sticking up high enough to catch the transmission or the oil pan. The track ended abruptly. They got out and looked into the slit in the earth. The tan four-wheeler was down seventy-five feet or so.

Du Pré pitched a rock down. Some of the birds flapped for a moment and then they settled again.

A trail wound back and forth down to the wreck. Du Pré started toward it. His moccasins slid some. He skated on the yellow earth. Benny came after him.

"You stay the hell up there, Benny," said Du Pré. "You puke on me twice, you know, you don't do that again."

Du Pré went on. He slid the last ten feet straight down, fetching up on the side of the Land Rover. All the glass bashed out of it. He looked in the back window. No blood. A dead hand hanging over the back seat.

Du Pré moved so he could see from the side. Man. Woman. Birds and animals had been at their faces. Skunk smell around. Blood on their clothes. Hair matted with blood.

He looked at the front seat.

Du Pré stood up.

"Benny!"

"Yah!"

"Two. You can call now."

Benny's face disappeared from view.

Du Pré went round to the other side. A couple shotguns in their cases spilled out of the open driver's door, a cooler leaking stinking water.

OK, Du Pré thought, where is this springer spaniel? We got a dog around here, maybe the coyotes haven't eaten him yet. Maybe the dog is dead where these people they were killed.

Du Pré scrambled back up. He pulled himself over the lip

of the slit, grabbing on to a sagebrush. Benny was sitting in his cruiser. Du Pré went to the driver's side and he leaned against the hood and smoked.

"Couple medical examiners flying in," said Benny. "We're gonna have a lot of help on this one. Jesus." He got out of the cruiser.

Du Pré offered him his tobacco and papers. Benny took them, though he'd quit smoking a long time ago.

"Benny, my friend," said Du Pré, "you quit now. You resign today."

Benny looked up.

"What will happen, you stay, they will think you are part of some group did this, they accuse you. They will try to scare you anyway, but don't stay, this one will maybe kill you. Please."

Benny nodded. "Susan said the same thing. But who will be Sheriff? They'll do the same thing to them, you know. I can't just leave my people to hang. I swore an oath."

"You didn't swear no oath to fight with them FBI," said Du Pré. "They don't care they get the right person, you know, just some person. I hear that they are better now. I hope they are, you know, but this will kill you. Then I got no place to take Madelaine, drink pink wine, play my fiddle."

Benny thought.

"I feel like a coward," he said.

"Hah," said Du Pré, "you no coward. Arresting kids, burgling, some fool swiping a car, drunk kill his wife, that is one thing. This is not that."

"I know," said Benny, "but who will do it? My deputies? I won't just dump this on one of them. I wanted this job, really."

"Not them," said Du Pré. "You are right."

"You?"

"No," said Du Pré. "We are going to have them FBIs here. Got to be someone they can't shove around, you know?"

Benny drew on his cigarette.

"We're little people here, Du Pré," he said. "No one has any money, or power. We're small ranchers, tradesmen, couple lawyers, don't have a doctor closer than Miles City. We're going to have a fucking army of FBI agents and newspeople and gapers and gawkers and folks wanting to write the whole story for the true-crime publishers. A zoo. And the meat's going to be some of our friends and neighbors. *We know these people, Du Pré, we know them.*"

Du Pré nodded.

"You come up with a name," said Benny, "and a good one, and I'll quit. If they agree to take it."

Du Pré nodded.

A siren, far off in the distance.

The helicopter was coming back, low.

"They are here already," said Du Pré.

"Who?"

"Them FBIs," said Du Pré. "That is not a crop duster." The chopper Du Pré had come in was owned by Taylor Martin, and pretty small.

This thing was much bigger, had jet engines on it.

Here come the fucking cavalry, Du Pré thought, as charming as usual. I think maybe they find their goddamned Little Bighorn, too.

They waited.

"I know the guy who will do this," said Du Pré.

"What?"

"Not kill those people, who will be the Sheriff."

"I think I do, too," said Benny.

"Bart," they both said.

11

"Perfect," Benny said. "He's richer'n God and he's been dried out a good long time and he don't take shit, we know that. But would he do it?"

"I ask him, he do it," said Du Pré.

My good friend. Years ago, he just a rich drunk but he is good now and people like and respect him. Very powerful man, the lawyer he got to come here, Charles Foote, got teeth way back to his asshole. Yes, that Bart, we need him now.

His lady, that pretty Michele, the cop, she dump him. She like that Washington, D.C. She crazy. He better do this, take his mind off that. She hate Montana, he was here long enough no place else good enough for him. She figure that out, too.

Life can be very sad.

The chopper began to circle the wreck, blowing dust all over Du Pré and Benny. They ducked into the cruiser.

"Pricks," said Benny.

"Well," said Du Pré, "you can count on them, for sure."

The big chopper set down and four men in dark suits jumped out into the cactus. They ducked under the blades and dashed toward Benny and Du Pré.

"I got a great idea," said Du Pré.

"What."

"Lock these doors," said Du Pré.

Benny shrugged and pressed the electric lock.

"Wait till they get here," said Du Pré.

"OK," said Benny.

"Then we give them the finger," said Du Pré.

Benny nodded.

"And then we drive home," he said.

They did and they did.

✦ CHAPTER 3 ✦

Benny swirled the whiskey in his glass and stared at the ice cubes in it.

"You got to do this, Bart," said Du Pré. "We help you, you know, but these people here, they need you now."

"Jesus," said Bart. "This is like handing me a stick of dynamite and tellin' me to suck on the end ain't lit."

He is talking Montanan pretty good there, Du Pré thought.

"We need you," said Benny.

"I don't understand," said Bart. "You resign and how do I get to be Sheriff?"

"County Commissioners appoint you," said Benny. "They can call an election, of course, or they can wait for a petition. But we need you right now."

Bart looked at Du Pré for a long moment. Du Pré looked at him.

"OK," he said. "I think I understand. I'm an outsider."

"Some people think you are an outsider if your great-grandfather wasn't born here," said Du Pré. "But not many. You are liked much. You dry out, you help, you work. How many people in trouble you help out? Many. You don't even tell me all. I hear it pretty quick, though, it is a small place."

"And what do I do when I find the people who killed these two idiots?" said Bart. "I arrest them and see them to trial. I will not do anything else. Those fools should have been spanked and sent home to Mother. Not murdered."

"No," said Du Pré, "they should not have been murdered. But you know these people, what happens, you press them too far, Bart."

Bart nodded. Old Booger Tom had probably shot the previous Sheriff. The Sheriff was shooting at Booger Tom. There was no evidence surviving and Booger Tom just looked amused when asked about it. Booger Tom made lovely horsehair hackamores and ropes and quirts; he'd learned to do that in Deer Lodge Prison. For killing two men.

I wonder what *that* was all about, Du Pré thought. All Booger Tom ever said about it was that they needed killing. They probably did.

"I'll stay on as a deputy," said Benny, "but there isn't anyone in the county who can do it but you."

Bart nodded.

"Thank you," he said.

"Thanks?" said Benny. "Jesus! This is going to be purely awful. I wouldn't blame you you pissed on my shoes."

Bart nodded.

"I'm going to call Guerdon Smith right now," said Benny. He went into the kitchen.

"It may get some worse, you know," said Du Pré. "I mean, they come here, cut the fences, shoot cows. Then there is that silly wolf thing, put them back in the Wolf Mountains. I think I will go to the hearing in Cooper, there, it is day after tomorrow. These people here have been here long time, you know, they don't like being told move on, we don't like you, got better idea for the place."

"I forgot about the wolf business," said Bart. "Are they here now, too?"

Du Pré shook his head. "Oh, I do not know. Sometime soon they will come, talk, go up in the Wolfs. I hope that they come *down*. You know my grandpapa, he kill the last wolves here in Montana, 1923, with that Don Stevens."

"A government hunter?" said Bart.

"Sometime, he was editor of that Great Falls paper, too," said Du Pré.

Benny came back, beaming. "I called Smith because he's the smartest, and he said . . ."

They waited.

Benny grinned. "He said he'd call the others and the whole business should be done today. Matter of fact, he said he'd come by the saloon and swear you in."

Bart nodded. "I hope I'm big enough to do this," he said. "I knew this would happen one day but I never thought I'd be the Sheriff who had to do it. Frankly, I am scared."

"Good," said Du Pré. "You weren't, you be pretty dumb."

"I suppose I'll need uniforms."

"We order ours from Chicago," said Benny. "Take a few days to get here. Nobody here's your size. You're a big man."

"Foote is going to *hate* this," said Bart. "I'll go and call him. You go on down to the bar, get some lunch. I'll be along in a moment."

Du Pré and Benny drove down Bart's drive and out onto the road.

"I never thought he'd do it," said Benny.

"Bart, he is bigger than you think," said Du Pré. "Trouble is, with lots of money, it is easier to throw it at life than take life's troubles. So you mostly never live, I think."

"He's got guts, for sure," said Benny.

There were a few people in the Toussaint Bar, having red beers and nibbling at the baskets of chips and pretzels Susan kept out for her customers.

Benny went round the bar, and then back into the

kitchen. When he and Susan finally came out her eyes were wet.

She reached across the bar top and took Du Pré's hand.

"Thank you," she said. "I was half out of my mind. I knew this was going to happen, too."

Du Pré grinned. "That Bart, he need to do this."

The door opened and Bart and Booger Tom came in. Bart looked a bit stunned. Booger Tom looked grim.

"I'se working for a lawman?" he said. "All my life I been a good dishonest cuss, honorable, never stole no horse nor cattle. Well, maybe some from them Eastern-owned ranches, I forget. I only robbed banks a couple times. Well, maybe four. I never killed anyone didn't really, really need it. And I wake up this morning, belch, fart, have my coffee, and ride into town with the goddamned *Sheriff?* I need a drink, bad."

"You never rode in with a Sheriff before?" said Du Pré. "You tell me that, look in my eye while you do."

"Plenty of times," said Booger Tom, "but it was some different . . ."

"You shoulda heard him scream," said Bart. "You'd think I scared him or something."

"Shit," said Booger Tom.

"Just don't do anything I'd have to arrest you for," said Bart. "You know how much I'd love it."

It is changing, Du Pré thought, something, like maybe my people when the buffalo were gone or they fled down here from the English. Left that Red River country, Canada, 1886.

The telephone rang. Susan went to answer it and she brought it to Bart.

Bart put it to his ear. He listened.

"I know, I know, Charles," he said. "I have to do this, though. I can't in conscience demand that you come. But I would deeply appreciate it. I'll buy you a thick down bag and plenty of caviar."

Lawyer Foote was abrupt.

Bart handed the phone back to Susan Klein.

"Well?" said Du Pré.

"He said he ought to have me committed," said Bart. "But he did quite understand and he would be here late this evening, and would like to be met at the Billings airport. He hates flying in little planes, especially at night."

"Madelaine and me, we go get him," said Du Pré, "if you want."

Bart nodded, then he shook his head no.

"Benny," he said, "I'm the Sheriff now, soon's Guerdon gets here with his Bible. So I would . . . what would you think of perhaps taking Susan to Billings? You could have—"

"We're outa here," said Susan. "Who'll tend bar?"

The door opened. Three men in dark suits came in. They peered a moment into the dark, saw Benny Klein, and came over to him.

"Special Agent Hansen," said one of them, a tall, dark-haired man, his mouth sneering, "and this is Special Agent Miller and that is Special Agent Houghton."

Benny nodded.

"Unusual," said Hansen, "to find a Sheriff in a bar when a case of this gravity has occurred."

"I'm not the Sheriff," said Benny.

"We were told he would be here," said Hansen.

"He's here," said Benny. "Bart? These . . . uh . . . folks seem to want to talk to you."

"Bart Fascelli," said Bart. He didn't get off his stool and he did not extend his hand.

"We need several things," said Agent Hansen. "Office space, telephones. Fax machines."

17

Bart nodded. "Then I suggest you go rent them," he said. He stood up. "This is my county. These are my people. You stupid cocksuckers fuck up once and I'll throw your asses over the line myself."

"Just a goddamned minute," yelled Hansen. "The Governor requested our assistance—"

"I don't work for the fucking Governor," said Bart. "So get him to rent some offices for you."

Guerdon Smith came through the door with a couple of the County Commissioners.

He walked up to Bart.

"You swear?" he said.

"Yup," said Bart.

Bart picked up the badge Benny had left on the bar top. He pinned it on. He stood in his old boots and torn jeans and stained leather jacket.

"Ever see *High Noon?*" he said. He grinned at Special Agent Hansen.

✤ CHAPTER 4 ✤

Du Pré stood at the back of the hearing room in Cooper. There were a bunch of very angry ranchers there, and some well-dressed young people in yuppie outdoor clothes, ugly colors and stupid buffalo designs on them.

"We will now listen to public testimony in the matter of reintroducing the gray wolf to the Wolf Mountains."

"We'll just kill the bastards!" shouted a weathered rancher.

The first speaker moved to the podium. A young woman

in hiking boots and multipocketed clothes.

"We need to restore the predators. . . ." she began. She stopped. There was a hail of cowshit landing on her and the Fish and Wildlife agents sitting at the long table on the dais.

She ducked and turned her back.

Something started hissing in the back of the room. Du Pré looked down at a stink bomb working up to good thick smoke. He ran for the door and made it through before the rest of the crowd caught on. They soon followed, choking in the fierce stench.

Du Pré laughed. He was wearing his Métis clothes, the high moccasins and Red River sash and hat, the doeskin pants and the loose shirt and leather jacket, buffalo with the fleece in. He rolled a smoke and lit it and watched the crowd sneeze and choke and bitch.

The high school auditorium would need to air a long time.

The Fish and Wildlife agents had been the last out. They coughed and cursed.

"Why don't you sons of bitches go bust poachers?" a ranchwoman yelled. "We aren't raisin' cattle to feed goddamn wolves, so these California bastards like Montana better. We like it just fine and we been here a hundred years."

Du Pré laughed. Jesus, he thought, they think they just march in here, tell us, hey, you get wolves back, we say fine? These wolves, they will not live very long, you bet.

The young woman who had tried to speak came up to Du Pré, wiping her eyes. She coughed a little.

"Excuse me," she said, "who are you?"

"Gabriel Du Pré," said Du Pré. "You did not get much chance in there."

She shook her head. "These stockmen, they just won't let us bring anything back. I've had cowshit thrown at me before."

19

Du Pré waited.

"Are you Indian, I mean Native American?" she said.

"Part Indian," said Du Pré. "Métis, French Cree Chippewa."

"Oh," she said. "What do you think?"

"Eh?" said Du Pré.

"About bringing the wolves back. It's a major medicine animal."

Du Pré laughed. "All animals are medicine animals," he said, "all of them four-footed, six-footed, eight. All."

"We came up yesterday and had a sweat with a Native American shaman," she said.

Du Pré grinned at her. "Maybe Benjamin Medicine Eagle?"

"Yes," she said. "Do you know him?"

"Oh, yes," said Du Pré, "I know him very well." Jesus. That little shit.

"It was very moving," she said. "We prayed for the return of the wolf."

Du Pré laughed.

"Why are you laughing?"

"His name is Bucky Dassault," said Du Pré. "He is a child molester, did time, Deer Lodge, he con his way to alcohol counselor, get fired from that, then he set himself up, shaman. He is a bad guy. How much he rip you off for?"

"Uh," she said, "oh, God."

"He didn't come here?" said Du Pré.

"Yes," she said, "he did, but then he said he had an appointment he had forgotten."

"No," said Du Pré, "I think that maybe he saw me."

"Oh," she said. Her eyes were red from the smoke.

"There are not so very many shamans," said Du Pré. "Medicine People are very rare."

"He sent us an ad," she said.

20

Du Pré nodded. An ad. Coupons, maybe.

"What do you think about the wolves?" she said.

"Well," said Du Pré, "it is a bad thing, bring them back, you have heard about the murders up near the Wolf Mountains, there."

"Those stockmen . . ." she said.

"You know, it is a very bad idea, cut fences, shoot someone's stock."

"They were friends of mine," she said.

"I am sorry," said Du Pré.

"I came here for them," she said. "We won't give up. But you didn't really say what you think."

"Um," said Du Pré. "My grandpapa, he hunt down the last two wolves in Montana, in the lower states here, with that Don Stevens. Old Snowdrift and Lady Snowdrift. Year before they kill them they find their pups, ship all but two of them to the Smithsonian. Don, he take one female pup and he train her, she was in some silent movies with a dog named Strongheart. My grandpapa, he raise a male but it get mean. He kill it. I still have the hide."

She was looking at him in horror.

"So if you stupid people do this I don't think that your wolves live very long. Very bad idea push these people around some. They don't take it."

The young woman reached in her pocket and she pulled out a tape recorder.

"I'm going to give this to the FBI," she said, "you bastard."

Du Pré laughed at her. He walked to his Rover and got in and drove off toward home.

Very strange, these people, he thought. The road home was a straight line north. They just come here, say everything has changed, because we told you so. I don't like this at all.

I got to keep any more of these fools from being killed.

21

That will not be easy. So stupid. They really want to clear everybody out from the Big Dry? Just tell them, go? Dig up the graves, your people, take them with you? We want a park here? Pretty crazy.

We got them FBIs, we got these people we never seen before. We got lot of change coming, maybe I have to go to Canada. That western Montana is very sad place. Strange people move in there, all alike mostly.

A coyote ran across far ahead of Du Pré's Rover.

Medicine animal there, for sure, Du Pré thought, he is some joker. Sometimes he catch himself up, get caught in his own jokes, yelp.

I go see Benetsee, Du Pré thought, old coyote joker there, see what he says. Be three in the morning I get there.

He reached under the seat and took up a pint of whiskey and sipped while the Rover shot down the two-lane highway. He had bought a pack of tailor-made cigarettes at the gas station. He smoked and drank and drove.

He shot past a Highway Patrol car lurking in the shadows where a county road came into the highway.

Du Pré sighed and flipped the switch and turned on his flashing lights and siren.

The Highway Patrol car slowed and turned off its light bar.

I liked Montana better before all those social workers, they take over the legislature.

Piss on 'em.

Du Pré's bladder sent its message. He slowed down and pulled off onto the verge and pissed in the road and got in and went on. Snow started to fall, fat flakes, so it wouldn't last long.

He pulled up to Benetsee's shack several hours later. He fished out a jug of bad wine from the back of the Rover and went up to the shack and banged on the door. Benetsee's old dogs woofed.

"Hey, old fart!" yelled Du Pré. "I got to talk to you!"
Du Pré waited.

Someone grabbed his shoulder. Du Pré whirled round.

"Hah!" said Benetsee. "You bring me some good wine there? Some tobacco? We drink, have a smoke, you come on in." He opened the door. A stench of old dogs and old man and dirty clothes and woodsmoke and stale wine hit Du Pré in the face. He rolled a cigarette and lit it and another for Benetsee. The old man poured himself some wine in a big dirty jar and he drank it in one long swallow.

"Pret' good wine," said Benetsee.

"You know all this bad news," said Du Pré.

"People got to be knowing how to fight, they make war," said Benetsee. "Pretty sad, kids, you know, they are dead now and lot of sadness. Parents lose kids, you know, they never get over it."

Du Pré nodded. "You got anything to tell me?" he said.

Benetsee drank a long drink. He puffed on his cigarette.

"These dead people, they played," he said. "All that they do, you know."

Du Pré nodded.

"They think, bring back the buffalo, forget the people. Bring back wolf, eat the buffalo, forget the people. Make it a place fools can play. Wear feathers. Maybe try to dance. Rub them crystals."

Du Pré had a slug of whiskey.

"Long time, you know," said Benetsee, "people been here. Before the whites, we hunt meat peoples, to honor them. We kill fur peoples to honor them, keep us warm. All the peoples make themselves for us, you know, and so we all live. Between the earth and sky. Keep each other strong."

Du Pré nodded.

"These new people they just play," said Benetsee.

"Yes," said Du Pré.

"So the earth hate them," said Benetsee. "I have never felt that. Earth hating anything."

Du Pré nodded.

"I got to go sleep," he said.

He went out and drove to Madelaine's.

✤ CHAPTER 5 ✤

Du Pré," said Madelaine, "I am worried now about you, do this, do that."

"Ah," said Du Pré.

"You got a real bad temper, these people they piss you off plenty. You don't kill none of them, eh?"

"OK."

Madelaine rested her head on the pillow again. They were lying in bed. Wind and sleet beat on the windows. The glass was steamed from their breath.

"You come on to Mass with me, yes?"

"No," said Du Pré. "I got to go see this FBI, Hansen, he want to talk to me about something. I tell him I be there at ten."

"I pray for your soul," said Madelaine. "I pray for this Hansen's ass."

Du Pré laughed.

"Pray, yours," he said, kissing her.

After, they sat in the kitchen. The television racketed mindlessly in the living room. Her teenage children watched it out of habit.

"You drop me church, pick me up?" said Madelaine.

"You be there pretty early," said Du Pré.

"Confession," said Madelaine.

All she got to confess she sin with me, these six years, the church don't like it. Oh well, that Father Van Den Heuvel, he give her a few prayers for the pretty words.

Du Pré dropped her off at the little cedar-sided church. He went on down the street and turned around and drove to the trailer park where the FBI had set up shop. They had to there because no one would rent to them, Bart wouldn't allow them in his building, and the owner of the trailer park was Susan Klein, who gave them a lot far away from anyone else and refused to rent it to them for more than one day at a time. She came for the rent every morning and always smiled and said how quickly they would be gone if they pissed her off.

The FBI had to truck a double-wide all the way from Miles City to work in. It was covered with satellite dishes and antennas.

Du Pré parked and he sauntered up to the trailer and went in.

Hansen looked up from his desk, slightly larger than those of his minions, scowling.

"You're late," he said.

"Kiss my ass," said Du Pré pleasantly. "Now what you want?"

Hansen glared at him.

"OK," said Du Pré, "you got fifteen seconds, say good morning, so I know I am not talking to an asshole. Then maybe I stay, we talk, you know."

"Good morning," gritted Hansen. "Have a chair. I'll get coffee."

"Not for me," said Du Pré. "I don't drink, place like this." He rolled a cigarette and dug a lighter out of his jeans.

"No smoking," said Hansen.

"OK," said Du Pré, "I go now."

"Shit," said Hansen. "Go ahead and smoke."

Du Pré nodded and lit up. Three other agents stopped what they were doing and came over, dragging chairs. They arranged themselves in front of Du Pré. Du Pré looked at them and he smiled sunnily.

"Who's doing this?" said Hansen. "Who killed those two people?"

"Ah," said Du Pré, "well, I don't know, I am sure that I know them, I know everybody, you know, but I do not know who."

"This is a small place," said Hansen. "You must have heard something."

"Dumb questions," said Du Pré. "This all that you got?"

Hansen snapped the pencil he was scribbling with.

"I go now," said Du Pré, getting up. He walked to the door and out and got in his Rover and backed up and turned round and went out to the street and off toward the Toussaint Bar.

Susan Klein was scrubbing the bar top with cleanser. The bleach smell cut through the old tobacco stink a little. She looked up when Du Pré walked in and she nodded.

"Stinking weather," she said.

Du Pré dug a beer out of the cooler and he put a dollar on the bar top. He popped the can open and he drank.

"Went to talk to them FBIs," he said. "Pretty dumb, them."

"They live in a different world, Du Pré," she said. "This one is real. Earth. Sky. People who know where they are. And it's part of them. They have a lot of fancy toys. Nobody will even speak to them. You know what will happen. We'll settle this ourselves."

Du Pré nodded. "A bad one, this," he said.

The TV crews had come, asked questions, got no answers, and left. Agent Hansen didn't have any, and Bart just said he'd talk with them when he had something to say.

When they learned that Bart was Bart Fascelli, a multimillionaire, working as a Sheriff in deepest Montana, they came pounding up his driveway, only to pound right back down it when Booger Tom shot a few times in the ground at their feet and then said that the next slugs would hit the TV cameras.

"I wouldn't waste a bullet on you," he said.

Tens of millions had watched him say that on international television.

There were newspaper reporters coming and going, and getting nothing. One of the victims was the daughter of a Congressman.

"That Bart he burn them back pretty good," said Du Pré, "like they are weeds, you know."

"Good," said Susan Klein. "God, did we need him. Poor Benny would have gone crazy."

Lawyer Foote had arrived. Bart had promptly deputized him and put him to work as spokesman. Newspeople working on him had the feeling that they were trying to crack a walnut with a banana.

The Governor had sent several state agents, who stayed about four hours. Bart called the Governor and they left.

Du Pré sipped his beer and watched the TV. News show.

No new leads on the Montana Murders, the news anchor said. She went on to other things.

"Maybe they figure we just shoot outsiders, they'll stay away," said Susan Klein.

Du Pré shrugged. That would be just fine.

Bart and Deputy Lawyer Foote came in, brushing snow and water from their uniform jackets. Foote's uniform fitted loosely; he had borrowed one from Benny Klein.

They came to Du Pré and Susan. She looked up.

"Coffee," said Bart.

"Brandy," said Foote.

"Drinking on the job," said Bart. "I reprimand you."

"Do that," said Foote.

Foote swirled the brandy in his snifter and smelled. He nodded. It was the only bottle of that brandy in Toussaint and the only snifter, for that matter.

"Them FBIs they haul me in there, ask a couple dumb questions," said Du Pré. "They ask me who is doing this. I tell them I am sure I know them but I do not know who."

"Wasn't the Stemples and it wasn't the Rosses," said Bart. "They were in Miles City when they were killed. Hell, it was two days later they found their cattle and the fences."

"They find anything in that car?" said Du Pré.

"No," said Bart. "Maybe the feds will find something, all the toys they got. But nothing I know of. Both of them shot in the head, a high-powered rifle, went right through. So no slugs, since they weren't killed there. No holes in the Land Rover."

"Where's the dog?" said Du Pré. "They had this springer spaniel?"

"Yes," said Bart, "I thought of that. But there's a lot of springer spaniels here, they live here, and more brought in."

"There was maybe a rabies tag in that Land Rover?" said Du Pré.

Bart shook his head.

"The vets?" said Du Pré. The two veterinarians in the county largely tended big animals.

"Neither one has seen the dog," said Bart.

"Well," said Du Pré, "that dog probably dead, too. Or maybe he run off and someone find him, cold and scared and hungry, and take him home. Dogs like that, expensive."

Bart nodded. He sipped coffee. They stared at the mirror a moment.

"If we can find the dog," said Bart, "what would it tell us?"

"Dogs," said Lawyer Foote, "do not usually talk."

"All we got right now," said Bart, "unless someone walks right in and says I did it, I'll tell you how, let me sign the confession."

"Someone probably will," said Lawyer Foote, "if not several. This is a pretty spectacular case. Attracts the unhinged, like politics."

"That uniform, it is not like you," said Du Pré to Lawyer Foote.

"No shit. I ordered some."

"Fancy tailor, Chicago?"

"Fancy tailor, London," said Lawyer Foote. "Got their start making uniforms for the likes of Lord Nelson."

Du Pré shrugged.

"I got to go," he said, "Just out to my car, a minute."

Get away a minute, Du Pré thought, think about that dog.

Du Pré stepped out into the storm. He heard children laughing and then three ran past. They had a dog with them, happily jumping up on them, splashing them with mud and water.

A springer spaniel.

Packy Jones's kids. The farrier.

Du Pré got into his car and started it. Jones's house was only a hundred yards away, but the weather was nasty. He drove slowly toward it.

✦ CHAPTER 6 ✦

She was just running along the road out west, there," said Packy. "Muddy and cold. I stop and open the door and she jumped in like I was her owner."

"Where you find her?" said Du Pré.

"Way the hell up on that back road cuts off to the Forest Service land," said Packy, "behind Tor Oleson's."

Thirty miles away.

Coyotes could chase her that far, a few hours. Didn't kill her, she must be coming into heat.

Those Oleson brothers didn't shoot them, they can't *see* that well. And they would not have heard anything. Du Pré had heard them try to play that fiddle. Hardänger stuff. Awful.

"She didn't have no collar on," said Packy, "and I thought some out-of-state hunter lost her. If anybody'd set up a howl for the dog I'd have give her back, but nobody did."

The kids came in with the wet, happy dog.

The spaniel came to Du Pré, shy and suspicious. She sniffed Du Pré's pant legs. He reached down and patted her head. She rolled on her back.

She had a tattoo on her belly, clear blue on the pink skin. A phone number. Du Pré scribbled it down.

Packy's TV blared in the corner. The murdered woman was to be buried this Sunday afternoon.

"The Montana Murders," the anchor droned. "Police suspect a serial killer."

For two people, same car, some serial killer. Huh? Du Pré thought. Catch these people, kill them, ditch them. Them FBIs don't got shit. Serial killer, hah.

"OK," said Du Pré, "Packy, you keep that dog, I don't tell anyone, them FBIs try to give a lie detector test to her, I think. Make her nervous, she would not pass. Lock the poor dog in a room, beat her with hoses or something. Yah, you keep her here. Don't tell nobody."

"I already told Susan Klein and Bart," said Packy, "in case someone was looking for the dog. I've had two run over, you know, it's like losing a child."

"Oh," said Du Pré. Why they not tell me about the god-damn dog?

Play a joke on Du Pré.

"Thanks," said Du Pré. "I see you. Nice dog."

Du Pré drove back to the bar. Bart was there, just sitting.

"Nice dog Packy's got there," said Bart, grinning. "And yes, it's the dog. The phone number is a tracing service. Tattoo your dog, someone finds it, they call this number. Belonged to the girl's boyfriend. I was afraid you'd tell the FBI about the dog," he went on. "Packy's kids love the dog and vice versa and the dog's happy and the dog can't read mug shots. So. They had anything, they wouldn't tell us. Screw 'em."

"You ready to play this afternoon?" said Susan.

Du Pré had forgotten. Another community supper and music.

My music. I have fun today, go chase down my neighbors later.

"I got to go and get Madelaine," said Du Pré. "We come back, she is making that lamb, rice, bay leaves."

"I love that woman," said Bart.

Du Pré picked up Madelaine at church and he dropped her at home and he drove off toward the benchlands. He saw the leaning trees around Benetsee's shack and a whiff of smoke coming up from the chimney. He drove up the rutted driveway and parked.

He knocked on Benetsee's door. The old dogs woofed, but the old man didn't come. He went around back to see if the old man was in his sweat lodge.

The fire pit was still glowing hot and the door flap was down in front of the sweat lodge.

Du Pré could hear the old man singing. He waited. The snow and rain were falling off. Some sunlight was punching down to the ground from the west.

31

Du Pré heard another car out front.

He walked round the house. One of the FBI cars.

Du Pré slipped back behind the sweat lodge. He squatted down behind a bush and waited.

"Some witch doctor," said Hansen, laughing loudly. He pounded on the front door.

"FBI!" he yelled. The old dogs woofed.

Du Pré whistled.

"There's someone around back," said one of the agents.

The three men came around the side of the shack. They looked at the sweat lodge. Not at the ground. Du Pré was fifteen feet away and his tracks led clearly to his hiding place.

The sweat lodge door flaps opened and Benetsee slid out. He stood up and looked at the three men in their city suits and city coats.

"I don't talk, Mormons," he said. "Go away."

"FBI," said Hansen. "You can either talk to us or we'll arrest you and take you in."

"Arrest?" said Benetsee. "For taking a sweat? Funny law, that."

"All right, you old asshole." One of the other agents lunged for the old man. His slick leather shoe soles wouldn't grip. He had to stop and get his balance back.

Benetsee grinned.

"You never find out," he said. "You can't see. Go home."

"That does it," said Hansen. "You know something. We're taking you in."

But he couldn't walk well.

Benetsee shrugged and he walked away a few steps.

An agent started to unbutton his coat.

Du Pré leaped for Hansen. He jammed his nine-millimeter in the agent's neck.

"You motherfucker," said Du Pré, "you got no right, do this to this old man. You bastards. You get your gun out slow, the others also. You drop them down. You got five seconds. Funny move, your brains are in Idaho."

"Do it," said Hansen to the other agents.

Plop. Plop. Plop.

"You get out of here now," said Du Pré. "I bring you your damn guns. You are so stupid. You do this, people, they will kill you here. Why you do this to an old man?"

Du Pré let go of Hansen.

"You bastards," he said. "You ever bother this old man you be very sorry."

"You will regret this, Du Pré," said Hansen.

"What you do?" said Du Pré. "You frame me, like you do? You guys, dumb and mean."

Du Pré walked them to their car. They got in and drove off. The FBI car's rear end swayed round; the driver didn't know how to drive in ice and snow.

There will be trouble, this, thought Du Pré. I do what? Let them shove old Benetsee around? He done nothing.

Du Pré reached in his Rover and turned on his radio.

"This is Du Pré," he said. "I need to speak to that Bart."

"You mean the Sheriff?" said the dispatcher.

God, I hate this woman, Du Pré thought.

"Yah," said Du Pré.

She patched him through.

"Three them FBIs they were here at Benetsee's," said Du Pré. "They push him around some, say they arrest him."

"Bastards," said Bart.

"So I shove a gun in that Hansen's ear," said Du Pré, "and I run them off."

"Gabriel," said Bart, "*please* don't do that sort of thing. *Please.*"

"Fuck them," said Du Pré. "That Benetsee, he don't do nothing."

Du Pré walked back up toward the sweat lodge. The flaps were shut again and wisps of steam were rising from the cracks in the lodge.

Du Pré shrugged and he drove down toward town.

Where the road suddenly dipped and turned he saw car tracks going off and over the side, down toward the creek bottom. Du Pré shot down the hill and pulled over and got out and walked to the edge.

The agent's car was upside down in the little creek. Hansen was crawling out of it.

Du Pré called the dispatcher and then he got out and he slid down the side of the hill.

Another agent had struggled out. The third one was hanging upside down in the car, unconscious. Du Pré got the seat belt unbuckled and he dragged the man out and up away from the car. The motor was still running and the gasoline fumes were heavy.

Hansen and the other agent crawled away on their hands and knees.

The car began to burn.

Sirens in the distance.

Hansen looked at Du Pré, hating him.

"Answer me a question," said Du Pré. "I am guessing."

Hansen stared at him.

"You are driving, and a coyote runs across the road."

Hansen nodded.

"It was funny," he said. "The coyote crossed and then it . . ."

Du Pré waited.

"It felt like something just shoved us over the side."

The ambulance stopped on the road above.

✦ CHAPTER 7 ✦

A coyote, eh?" said Deputy Lawyer Foote. "Life is a strange business."

Du Pré nodded. They were sitting in the saloon, eating cheeseburgers and drinking beer. The fire roared in the glass-fronted woodstove.

They were the only two people left in the bar. Susan Klein had left, saying they should pull the door shut after them. The potluck had been a success. They always were, and Du Pré had fiddled like he always did.

"Wonderful music," said Foote. "Is it Celtic? It sounds like some I have heard, Irish and Scottish."

"It is that," said Du Pré. "We got some Indian, some French, some Scot. We some stew, us."

"Did you tell me what the Métis are?" said Foote.

"We the voyageurs. Some French they come, Scot, Irish, all them Catholic, with the Black Robes, them Jesuits. Very tough priests, them Jesuits. And they marry Indians and here we are. Some of us, we live on the reservations, some of us don't, most of us are gone, part of what America mostly is, you know. Indians call us white, whites call us Indians. So we are the peacemakers, catch all the shit from everybody."

Foote laughed.

"You weren't too peaceful with Hansen," he said. "God, that could have been trouble for you."

"Why they do that to an old man?" said Du Pré.

"No one here will talk to them," said Foote. "They are very used to solving things. With a murder, you know, if you don't solve it quickly the chances of solving it ever are small. And they are under great pressure to solve these cases. So three of them are in the hospital and now we get three more. Or more. I expect they will lean on you."

Du Pré nodded. Stick a gun in an FBI neck, they take it personally.

"I hope they don't any of them get killed," said Du Pré.

"Oh, God," said Foote, "that would mean we would have hundreds of them here. I have been able to forestall their . . . overcrowding . . . so far. The political reality is that fatuous rich kids perceived as defenders of the environment are thought much more valuable than the backwards sixth-generation ranchers, who I seem to remember stand or fall on how well they take care of the grass. The people who have lived here for a century or more are most independent. They don't resent outsiders interfering with them. They refuse to tolerate it at all. It worries me. A great deal."

"Worry me, too," said Du Pré. "The first time, you know, some FBI pulls a gun on a rancher, that rancher's wife, she will just blow that FBI guy away like a gopher. Them FBIs, they don't know how to act, they need to go away, let me and Bart and Benny and the others figure this out. They make things, you know, much worse."

"There is a lot of loose talk about a conspiracy," said Foote.

"You think these ranchers get together, say, these fools come here, we wait for them, shoot them, maybe next Wednesday at ten at night? Paugh. No."

"Please explain," said Foote.

"OK," said Du Pré. "These fools come here, but it is not their land, you know. They drive around it, they think, well, this is very empty land, nobody on it. But I make you a bet. You, Lawyer Foote, you go on out when the season for deer it is over. You shoot one deer from the road. You see how long it is before the game warden is with you. No, I know what happen. These people are young, city people, can't see much here. They are here, cut these fences, shoot cows, they want a nice place to play in. They are scared, too. So they are on a dirt road, don't see nobody around, they drive slowly back and forth, for Chrissakes. They maybe smoke a joint, drink a little, helps some. They are out there after dark, driving around, headlights, slow. How far can you see headlights, this country? Oh, fifty miles. So someone has seen them, they have come, they are wondering, what in the hell are these people doing out here, anyway? Then those dumb kids, they get out of their expensive four-wheel-drive, they go cut fences, shoot some cattle. Whoever is watching them says, Jesus Christ, enough is enough. So whoever is watching these fools, they grab a gun and they shoot them, they are so mad. They just kill them."

Foote nodded. "I see," he said. "I suppose out here, empty as it looks, someone is always watching."

"Always," said Du Pré. "Now, this person who shot those two stupid kids, they are pret' mad at the bunny-huggers already. Environmentalists, they just march in here, say, you are bad people, this is our land now, get off it. Jesus Christ, what they expect? Free beer? Shit."

"They don't drink," said Foote. "They expect free designer mineral water and fat-free cheese. God, everybody who lives here has guns. I know that the owner is a local if there is a gun rack in the pickup. Full of guns. Guns which it is illegal even to own, I'd bet, too."

Du Pré thought about the machine pistol in his attic. The one Catfoot, his papa, had brought home from the war. MP-40. Schmeisser. It worked just fine. Someday Du Pré might need it.

"Tell you a story," said Du Pré. "It is the early sixties and this Federal Commissioner, Aviation, is flying across Montana in a plane, he sees another plane flying along with him, it comes up suddenly. The pilot is wearing a cowboy hat and dark glasses. Pilot grins. He fires off the machine guns, the twenty-millimeter cannon, so that the Commissioner knows they work, tracers, you know. He does a flip over the Commissioner's plane, so that he sees there are no identity numbers. It is painted like sagebrush and rock and grass. Commissioner, he goes crazy, hundreds of people looking for that plane, they never find it. It is still out there somewhere, in some rancher's barn. Rancher, he figures, he's had enough of that Washington, D.C., he strafe it."

"Hmmm," said Foote. "What kind of plane was it?"

"Old P-thirty-eight Lightning," said Du Pré. "You know, it is very fast for a propeller plane. I read about it. Somebody out there, cowboy hat, he owns it, loves it, keeps it oiled up and ready."

"Jesus," said Foote, "I think I see what you're saying."

Du Pré fetched more whiskey and the brandy bottle from the bar. He sat back down and he rolled a smoke. Foote lit one of his long black cigars and he leaned over and lit Du Pré's cigarette.

"I see now why you wanted so to have Bart take the Sheriff's job," said Foote.

Du Pré nodded.

"Times will change but these people will not," said Foote, "and they won't run or bend or give an inch."

"No," said Du Pré, "they will not. You know what is needed here, I think, is some FBI from here, knows these people. Lead these agents, make them not get themselves killed. Because they will work very hard and that is where it will end, I know, sure as hell, and when it happens and they send more and more get killed, that will be all."

"I'll see what I can do," said Foote.

Foote took his brandy and went off to a corner and made two phone calls.

Ah, thought Du Pré, I am friend to a guy, he can call Washington, D.C., at three, the morning, and someone will answer.

Foote sat down, cigar in his hand, brandy snifter in the other.

"Done," he said, "if they don't screw it up. I expect them to screw it up, but not too much."

Du Pré rolled another smoke and he lit it and he looked up at the blue tendrils rising.

"Things changing," he said, "much change. A time that is bent and maybe breaking. Old Benetsee, he listen to the earth, you know, he say it is speaking to him and never has this way before."

"He has a truly terrible moral force," said Foote. "I can't quite understand how those agents could have treated him so; my impulse is to bow. Never had that before. So a coyote ran in front of the car and then an unseen hand pushed the car over the bank. Curious."

Du Pré nodded. His power, reach a long way. Du Pré remembered the River of the Whale.

"Yah," said Du Pré, "I feel him all the way east in Canada, that mess with Lucky, few years ago." When I kill a man, have to, old Benetsee he see it coming.

"It is possible," said Foote. "And I should warn you, that the FBI may send someone from the West who left because he hated it and he will be real glad to make it worse."

"Shit," said Du Pré.

"What do you mean by changing?" said Foote.

"Last time it changed this much, it is 1886, the Métis rise up in Canada, they fight the English, poor mad Louis Riel he talking to Jesus and Jesus say, hang two English. Then Louis Riel he don't let his little general, Gabriel Du-

39

mont, defeat them English and so the Métis they lose and the priests betray poor Louis Riel and the English hang him. Some the Métis, they come down here, North Dakota, the buffalo are gone and they have nothing, they got maybe a Red River cart, hoe, ax, couple horses. Nine children, probably. They stay here, Indians hate them call them white, whites hate them call them Indian. But we live."

Foote nodded.

They smoked.

"Now these new people come, they say everybody here is bad people, you go away now, we want to play on your land. Bring back wolves. Bring back buffalo. But they don't know, these people."

Foote nodded.

"So these people here, first they don't understand, they are some confused. Then they get very angry, when they do understand."

Du Pré blew smoke at the ceiling.

"And then?" said Foote.

"Then they say, it is a good day to die."

"I have heard that line in a lot of movies," said Foote.

"Yah," said Du Pré, "well, that is silly Hollywood saying it. But I tell you something, I just think of it. It means you, too."

Foote nodded and waited.

"You live this country, a time," said Du Pré, "and you walk on it and you listen to it talk with you, you listen to the many peoples—rocks, trees, four-leggeds, six-leggeds, winged peoples—you are Indian. It will happen, you don't know it, maybe you are a rancher, *hates* Indians. But it take you."

"I see," said Foote.

"We got to stop this," said Du Pré. "But me, I do not for sure know how."

❖ CHAPTER 8 ❖

Du Pré and his daughter Jacqueline's husband, Raymond, were sitting on a fence rail smoking. They had just signed off on a double load of calves headed for feedlots and tables out east. The diesel engines of the trucks taking them were fading to nothing in the distance. It was one of the warm November days, golden light and the air so clear things seemed closer than they were.

Du Pré stared up at the Wolf Mountains.

"Well," said Du Pré, "them assholes want to put them wolf back there, I guess I go kill them like my grandfather did."

"I help," said Raymond.

"No, you don't," said Du Pré. "I tell you something, you do this kind of thing ever, you do it alone and you don't talk about it."

"You just talked about it," said Raymond.

"Yah," said Du Pré, "well, now I don't got to do it. Someone else do it, you bet."

A pheasant flushed from the thick weeds in the creek bottom over the road. Then another.

"Someone down there chasing them," said Du Pré. "Wonder who?"

"What you ever find out about that dog Packy got?" said Raymond.

"Oh, he belong to that murdered woman's boyfriend.

End of that, it was just a call-in service, find a lost dog, call eight hundred."

The springer spaniel broke cover and ran down again into the weeds. Du Pré looked off east and saw Packy coming, shotgun across his chest, high. A pheasant flushed in front of him and he shot it, one smooth motion, boom, a puff of feathers.

Packy waved and then he disappeared, down behind a hill.

Du Pré heard a car coming, pretty fast. Drive like they are from here, he thought.

A tan government car topped a rise and then dipped out of sight. It came up again, still roaring, then began to slow down three hundred yards or so away. The car slowed and stopped.

A woman got out, standing up in one smooth motion. She had gray hair with white streaks in it. Dressed in jeans and boots and a worn rough leather jacket. She reached into the car and pulled out a stained hat and put it on.

She walked up to Du Pré and Raymond, chewing slowly.

She nodded. Clear blue eyes, lines around her mouth and eyes. About forty. Very lean. Horsewoman.

"Gabriel and Raymond," she said. "Told I'd find you here." Her accent was Montana, down deep. "I'm an FBI agent. In charge of this mess. Name's Corey Banning."

Gabriel and Raymond took off their hats and shook hands with her. They put their hats back on.

"I thought so," she said, grinning. "Now, I got a favor to ask of you, hope that it won't piss you off too much. I need to talk with Mr. Du Pré here, and Raymond, if you could maybe drive my car back to town we'll pick it up later."

"I got to go anyway," said Raymond. "I let Gabriel bring you my house, pick it up. Nice to meet you."

He walked over to the pool car and drove away.

"Just broke a bunch of regulations," said Corey Banning, "so fuck 'em."

Du Pré went to his Rover, got out a half-full bottle of whiskey, came back. He offered it to her.

"Obliged," she said, taking a sip.

Du Pré had a good slug.

"Whew," said Corey Banning. "Now, murder is not, as you know, a federal crime, so I am here to prove who violated their civil rights, which since they are dead I think must have happened. I ain't going away till I find out who, why, where, when, and all that good stuff. Now, unfortunately us folks at the FBI have a very poor reputation in the courtesy department and I just made it very clear to the three guys who came with me and who already hated my guts that they got to sir and ma'am and not shit in the punch bowl. Or someone'll blow their fool heads off."

"Good," said Du Pré. "Now I feel some better. I thought that maybe we have a war, you know?"

"Well, yeah," said Corey Banning, "it was headed that way. Now you and me, we know what happened. The little dummies thought no one was watching them and someone of course was and they lost their tempers some and killed them. That's against the law and further it ain't right."

"Yah," said Du Pré.

"Now I'm going to find these folks," said Corey Banning, "every goddamned one of them, and I'm going to see them tried and put in prison. You can go to the bank with it. And if you or Bart—nice guy, I like him—or Benny Klein screw up, withhold information, or break the law I'll do the same to you. Only fair to warn you. I got a job to do and further I happen to like the job."

Du Pré laughed.

"So I want to hear from you today all that you know. Everything. Now, we'll just sit here if you don't mind smoking and having a drink now and again, putting a little smile on, till all my questions are answered. I like answered questions, I hang around till I get them. Real pain in the ass. Not too bright, sometimes three, four days later, I think, now I didn't like that answer, I come back, see if it's changed any. Or maybe, I think, I asked that question wrong, there."

"OK," said Du Pré. "I am very glad you are here, you know why? Now, that Benny he quit, he don't want to arrest his good friends and neighbors and so he do that. Bart, he swallow hard and then he say, well, I will do this job best I can."

"Pretty strange," said Banning. "Guy's got more'n a hundred million dollars, dried-out drunk living in the ass end of nowhere to begin with, and suddenly he's the law. Good guy?"

"Yah," said Du Pré, "I think he be a very sad guy before this is over, but he is a good guy."

"Sad families just buried their kids, Du Pré," said Agent Banning. "Those kids were too dumb to walk and chew gum all at once, but they still didn't need killing. Even if they did we don't do things that way anymore."

Du Pré shrugged.

"Like that guy you killed in New York," said Agent Banning. "You do recall your old friend Lucky? Bad guy. You did the right thing, mind you, and I can say that because we never got any evidence and you ain't going to dance on in and confess and say please hang me. But I know that you did it and of course you know it's against the law and out of fashion. Even here."

Du Pré looked at her.

Ah yes, she is something, this one, he thought.

"Now," said Banning, "the Rosses and the Stemples they come up to you and tell you about their cut fences and

44

dead cattle, you're playing at the bar—I love that music, I'll
be there next time, you bet, you bet—they got good alibis
and so it ain't them. Now, you aren't exactly a cop so I
suspect you're too smart to be one which I admire but
when you get back you're going to find ol' Bart there at the
bar with a badge for you on account of how I asked him so
nice and blinked my baby blues at him and waved my ass
under his nose. Actually, I just told him it would be easier
and he agreed."

"How long you talk to him he say that?" said Du Pré.
"Just want to know?"

"Oh," said Agent Banning, "about two minutes, I
guess, you know how I get? Scream, foam, bite things.
Told him I'd cut a deal with him, he slaps a badge on you,
I don't let those three pussies they stuck me with out of the
trailer, they can sit in there, pull each other's dicks, answer
the phone, I don't care. Useless as the tits on a slab of bacon
but the main office is always trying to help. Bunch of fucking social workers, don't want the poor little things out on
the street. I'll get rid of them soon enough but you know
they'd just get themselves killed I let them go outdoors,
and how would I feel? Actually, I wouldn't really give a shit
but it's against the law which I do care about so I got to
arrest more people and then they get pissy, they think I'm
making work for myself so I can stay here. You know how
their tiny little minds work. Hardly at all. They're so dumb
all I got to do is water 'em once a week, sprinkle a little
bullshit on 'em."

Du Pré howled.

"Yeah," said Agent Banning, "I do a great stand-up rou-
tine, don't I? Now I got to have your help. I just have to
have it. You ever want one thing so bad you can just taste
it? Run your credit card over the edge getting it? Do that?
Well, I just got to have you, Deputy Du Pré, just until it's

45

over. I just won't settle for less, you know."

"OK," said Du Pré, "but we got to let Benny off this one. He's too kind a guy for this job."

"Already done," said Banning. "I talked to his wife and we agreed on it, I don't want anybody hurt don't have to be, and he'd just fuck up and I'd have to bust him."

Du Pré nodded.

"Slug of that, please," said Special Agent Banning. "Christ, I lend government property, drink on the job, show disrespect for my superiors. Oughta report myself but I don't feel like it." She had a good pull of the whiskey.

"Now my first question," said Agent Banning, "is also my last question until I think of another, which may take a bit of time."

Du Pré waited.

"How far is it to this Medicine Person," said Agent Banning. "I have some gifts of respect in a bag over by your Rover there, and I would very much like to meet him."

Du Pré looked at her.

"We go there," he said. "He is called Benetsee."

"Ben-et-see," said Agent Banning, slowly. "Mr. Benetsee."

"No," said Du Pré, "just Benetsee."

"OK," said Banning, "I won't mister him."

✤ CHAPTER 9 ✤

But Benetsee wasn't there. The sweat lodge was cold and empty and no smoke came from the chimney. The dogs were on the front porch of the shack. There was a pile of gnawed bones and scrap meat a little ways away and they could drink from the creek, eat the scraps, and sleep in the warm place under the porch.

Agent Banning scratched their ears.

"I think he's watching us," she said, "either from that bunch of rocks over on the ridge there or the willows just across the creek. You mind we wait a bit? Actually, we wait a bit. I got to talk to him. Oh, well. Tell you what, I'll just bet you there's a chopping block back there, and I'll just go and put this wine and tobacco and meat back on it and then come back and we just sit here on the front porch, have us some more of that whiskey and I'll bum a couple smokes off you and we'll wait."

"I am supposed to meet my Madelaine, hour or so," said Du Pré. "I got to go then."

"Actually, you don't," said Banning. "I talked to her, see, she was in the bar when I talked to Susan Klein and I said, look, I got to do this with your Du Pré, sorry about that. She said fine, tear your ass off if I needed to."

Yah, thought Du Pré, that sound like my Madelaine, all right. She think this is funny.

"So we'll just wait till he comes. We'll wait all night and all day tomorrow and all week and still be here when the snows fucking melt but I just got to talk to this Benetsee and I won't have it any other way or with anyone but you."

She walked round back and put the wine and meat and tobacco and a small knife on the chopping block. She pulled a twist of sweet grass out of her jacket and lit it and set it on a stone on the ground.

"Uncle!" she yelled. "I must speak with you! You can help me! Please, Uncle!"

"Good," said Du Pré.

"I hear he's a very sacred person," said Banning, "and I will not be a smart-ass with him. My mother had kidney cancer and the Mayo Clinic told her to go home and die quietly. So I took her to a person like this Benetsee and she is seventy-six and on the third husband now, the other two died."

"Oh," said Du Pré.

"My daddy was a test pilot," she said, "you know how that goes. Lost him when I was three. Next one was a drunk and a lawyer and you know how *that* goes."

"OK," said Du Pré. He waited. "Who is the third?" he said.

"A really good guy," said Banning. "A blind blues saxophone player, wonderful man. Blind and black. They live in Paris."

Du Pré laughed.

"No shit," said Banning. "Great guy. She's wonderful. Sends me these frilly things. Tells me to get married."

"And?" said Du Pré.

"Well, I got married the one time but it didn't work out," said Banning.

"What happened?" said Du Pré.

"I shot the son of a bitch for pissing out the bedroom window. It bothered me, so I became an FBI agent so I wouldn't do that again."

There is a true story in there somewhere, Du Pré thought. I chew on it long time maybe I guess it.

"Now, these people who shot the kids they get murder two," said Agent Banning, "'cause I don't think they were thinking about it till they saw the stupid little bastards cutting the fences and shooting the cattle, and you know we got to stop this because otherwise it's going to be a sport, you know, shoot anything walks funny, eats tofu, or carries around a flag with baby seals on it. You know, I know, small-town West is going to die, our wonderful government is going to kill it off. They like doing that to small cultures, did it to the Indians and now it's us but it's how history moves, and beef is a bad word now and we live in a democracy and we got a very small voice. Oh, by the way, when they release those damn wolves up there they'll last about two hours and I know that and I don't care. I don't want to hear it, or about it. That's Fish and Wildlife crap, doofuses. They pulled me off some drug murders, Jackson Hole, to send me up here. God, that place is unbelievable. Good place for a nuclear accident, you ask me. Well, we had this when it was good."

"Yah," said Du Pré, "it was. I don't think that we lose it, though. This is just one bad moment."

"Hope so," said Banning, "but I don't think so. Well, we had it when it was good and I actually feel for the poor little bastards who came here to save everything, bring back the woolly mammoth and such. It was gone when they got here because when they came they came in a tide and they just swamped it. All the drinking water in the Rockies is poisoned now with giardia. Thank you, backpackers."

Du Pré laughed.

How many more people dead before this is over, he thought sadly. It came on him suddenly. He looked down at his feet.

Banning held the whiskey bottle in front of Du Pré.

"We got to do this," she said. "It's ugly enough now, Gabriel. Really ugly. And you know how bad it could get."

"Yah," said Du Pré, "I am not going to enjoy being a good guy this time, if I am."

"Gray hats, for sure," said Banning. "I give that old bastard about five minutes before he comes round the shack. I hope I didn't leave him too much wine."

"Not possible, leave him too much wine," said Du Pré. "You know these persons. I got more, he wants it. He is some old man. I sometimes want to break his dirty old neck, but then I think, sometimes he don't know the answers, just the riddles."

"Case you are wondering," said Banning, "I just want to ask for his help and he'll do it or not and I'll take what he gives me and it's all right, whatever."

"I knew that," said Du Pré. "I tell you I help. You are right, it was not right, kill those people. I wish it had not happened. I wish for many things in my life. I wish it happened someplace else, I wish my leg was broke. I wish much. But I help you. I will find myself in front of somebody I went to school with, hunted with, drank with, maybe someone who saved my life, this country almost take it few times. I don't like this."

"Thanks," said Banning. "I didn't know if you could fly high enough to see it. I am truly grateful."

"I have lived here always," said Du Pré. "Little time, the army, but that is all. My papa is brand inspector, and when he is killed I am. I got one daughter here with many children, the other she is finishing up her doctor's degree, at Yale. That Bart, he pay for her everything. But me, I am here, I don't know too much else. Now I got to go to my life, my friends, cut some of them out, put handcuffs on them, see them off to bad prisons, have their families hate me forever. I don't like it."

Banning nodded.

"I say I help you and I will, unless this Benetsee he tells me I can't. I am sorry, I give you my word and then I think of this. If he says no I go away."

"He won't say no," said Banning. "Whatever is bad now will only be worse if you don't help and he will know that. A bad time, it's here, and we have to deal with it. Your Madelaine told me something about you, Du Pré, she knows you well. She said you'd charge hell with one bucket of water. I ain't heard that for thirty years."

50

The old dogs stirred. They got up and woofed wheezily.

"Benetsee!" said Du Pré. "We need you, my friend."

The old man was behind them on the porch.

"Some good wine," said Benetsee. "I like maybe a good smoke. You roll it thick, yes?"

Du Pré did. He handed it to the old man and held out his lighter to him. Benetsee drew deeply on the cigarette.

Benetsee knelt down and held the smoke in front of Banning. She took it and had a long drag.

"You got a good spirit," said Benetsee, "falcon spirit. Pretty swift, little too sure sometimes, get you in trouble, crash into things."

"Yes, Uncle," said Banning.

Benetsee moved down the steps. He squatted in front of her and he looked at her face for a long time. He finished his cigarette.

"You better be my daughter," said Benetsee. "I can help you more."

She nodded. "A great honor," she said.

"No shit," said Benetsee. "You going to need it. Now, Falcon Woman, you got more to do, you know."

Banning's head snapped up. She looked levelly at Benetsee.

"Coyotes sing early this morning," said Benetsee. "They tell me sad things."

No, Du Pré thought, please, no more.

Benetsee stood up and he tugged at Banning's sleeve till she rose and she followed him.

"People, last night they let wolves out up there. They sneak them in three days ago, pen them, last night they let them loose. Eight wolves. Four people up there with them."

"Oh, God," said Banning.

"Two wolves left now," said Benetsee. "They get lucky, run right."

51

"The people?" said Banning.

"Coyotes say two wolves left," said Benetsee.

Agent Banning looked up at the Wolf Mountains, bright with snow. A thin line, gray as the lead of a pencil scraped over paper, stretched east from the tops of the peaks.

"It's going to snow like hell up there," said Banning.

Shit, Du Pré thought. Shit. Goddamn it.

Six.

✤ CHAPTER 10 ✤

Who do we know that can go up there on snowshoes very quietly and kill four people and six wolves and then come back down quietly and not leave a fucking trace?" said Bart. "The bastard even dug the slugs out of their heads. Chopped them open with a hatchet and fished around in their brains till he got the slugs and then off he went singing a happy song. Probably twenty-two hollow-points. He is thorough, he goes back to his home, fires up the old cutting torch, melts down the barrel, and leaves us here with our dicks in our ears."

Du Pré tossed a dart at the dartboard. It had a photograph of the Governor on it. Very tattered.

"Ah," said Du Pré, "forty people could do all that, you know. But this one it is different. This time that person was hunting those Fish and Wildlife assholes. Maybe more, Bart, they were not even from this place."

Bart nodded. It was snowing like hell outside.

"He'll be easy," said Corey Banning. "Whoever did this did it in cold blood. Means they like it, they'll do it again. They'll fuck up."

Du Pré sighed.

"What we need to do today," he said, "we maybe go down to the bar there, drink some, I play a little fiddle, lot of people there, the weather is nice bad, just snowy, not too cold, they not got much to do, don't do much more than feed the cattle, take a couple hours, we just be there, maybe someone say something."

"I got some paperwork," said Banning. "I'll see you later. Check in on my little helpers. What a priceless little bunch of peckerheads. I wonder what their mothers did to them after they cut their balls off."

Bart laughed.

She went out, cussing.

"What a lady," said Bart.

Du Pré shrugged.

"We going to have to get lucky, this one," he said. "Nobody see anything, hear gunshots, nothing. No trucks, cars they see. They blind, deaf. That bunch of people dead in the mountains, it will not take long to find out who did it. But maybe never on the first two."

"That guy who did kill those four people," said Bart, "he might have done the others. If, like Corey says, we can get him first, he might crack. Our best bet."

One fucking crack, Corey Banning had said, one crack and we get a wedge in and then we go. Just one crack. Or heat it up and pour water on it and see what flakes off. Or go ask Benetsee what he's seen lately. But find that crack, now.

They drove to the Toussaint Bar. The place was packed and smoky. Susan was mixing drinks and Madelaine was in the back frying hamburgers.

Du Pré looked at the prime rib sign. So it was Friday night.

He waved at the accordion player from Cooper and the guitarist. They had their instruments out on the little stage.

Du Pré went back out to the Rover and got his fiddle. He took it in and opened the case and left it sitting on top of an amplifier left over from the country band, to warm up so it would stay in tune.

Susan shoved a glass of soda at Bart and a double whiskey at Du Pré and she bustled off.

The air was hot, damp, and close. Du Pré took off his jacket and untied the kerchief at his throat. He tossed his hat and jacket on the stage and he sat on a stool sipping whiskey.

I know every face, this room, he thought. One of you, two of you, who did this thing.

I know my people. I make a list, I write them on it, I cross them out one by one, I do this and something it will go click and then I will know before I know. I will find this one, have to smell it.

Like a coyote. Coyote looks for things aren't right. Trap there, a circle that is something's eye, something to eat. Way I track. Look for something that is not right.

Packy lurched up to Du Pré. He was very drunk, his eyes bleary. He deserved to be, pulling shoes off horses fifteen hours a day for six weeks.

"They got the sonsofbitches this morning," said Packy.

"Huh?" said Du Pré.

"Them fucking wolves. They came down to Stemple's feedlot and he got 'em, two shots."

Good, Du Pré thought. Now if they don't do it again we maybe don't get anybody more killed.

Who is a trapper?

Fur market is down so bad no one does it.

Du Pré remembered sending his furs to Sears, Roebuck and getting things back for them, thirty years ago.

Used to do it, till the bobcats got cut back so far, used to be you got three hundred fifty for a bobcat pelt.

Bill Stemple. Packy, till he got stove up so bad. Draft

horse kick him, then step on the other leg. Gets around pretty good, though. And those two brothers, the St. Francis boys. They're forty. Never married. Folks are dead.

Marcus and George St. Francis.

Not Bill Stemple, he would not do that, he shoot the wolves for sure, hell, anybody do that. Spit in their faces, those fools want them here. Packy is too sweet a guy and he can't get up there.

St. Francis boys both trap once, they are of this country, they know it, I know them, they are very quiet.

Kind of crazy, I always think, Du Pré thought. Can't think why I think that.

Du Pré saw them across the room, leaned up against the wall. They were dressed in stained brown overalls and coats, farmer caps, boots with rubber bottoms and leather tops. Big guys, strong. Played basketball, high school.

Or it is somebody over the other side of the mountains, north, they are doing it.

Du Pré made his way across the room to the St. Francis brothers. They looked at him curiously.

I don't think that I have spoken to them, twenty years, thought Du Pré. But I am remembering something.

What?

Bart and Banning had talked to them and they got nothing.

Suddenly Du Pré remembered. Both of them had had some trouble as kids. They were twins, the kind that look different from each other.

Set some cars, a house on fire, got sent to the state school, Pine Hills. Kept to themselves.

Fuck it, thought Du Pré, I am tired of playing by the rules.

He stood in front of them. They smiled at him. Shook their heads.

"Bart and Banning didn't think of something," said Du

Pré, "but I did. You guys shot those people up in the mountains. Left some witnesses."

The brothers looked at him blankly.

"Best place for those wolves come down was yours," said Du Pré, "but they would not. They smell you, go to Stemple's."

"You're crazy," said George.

"I am that," said Du Pré. "I am also right, you know. I be along."

He walked away.

The St. Francis brothers left right away.

"Hey, Bart," said Du Pré, leaning over close to Bart's ear, "those St. Francis brothers, they probably killed those people up in the Wolfs."

"I talked to them, Banning talked to them," said Bart. "They both had stories and stuck to them. You know what ranching is. Pretty lonely life. Half the county couldn't come up with one witness to say they were anywhere in particular on a given day."

"Them wolves come down to Stemple's?" said Du Pré. "They should have come to St. Francis place. Closer, and they got some sheep. They smelled the men who killed the wolves up there, Bart, so they went over another entire mountain. Don't make sense. It was snowing so hard then, wolves are like everybody else, you know, they got reasons to do things."

Bart nodded.

"I don't think I can get a warrant on that," he said.

Corey Banning came in. Eyes followed her across the room. She ignored them.

Bart and Du Pré waited.

When she got to them Du Pré told her what he thought. She listened, nodding.

"They kill animals?" she said. "Set them on fire, torture

56

them? Were they bullies, beat up smaller children, laugh while they did it?''

Du Pré rubbed his eyes. Something, long time ago, what?

A dog. It had a dog in it.

Long time ago. Come on, come on.

Snap.

Du Pré had been driving by the grade school and he had seen some kids outside gathered around a dog that had been killed by a passing car.

The children had either been crying or laughing.

All but the St. Francis brothers were crying. They smiled. They had laughed.

Them?

Maybe.

✤ C H A P T E R   1 1 ✤

B art kicked his official desk in his official office.

"I don't fucking *believe* it," said Bart. "The ultimate goddamned alibi, for Chrissakes, I can't stand it."

The St. Francis brothers had both been in jail when the murders occurred. For beating up a whore in Billings. They were out on bond. They had spent a lot of their lives out on bond. The whore probably wouldn't press charges.

"How many times that happen?" said Du Pré.

"They're forty-two," said Bart. "I would guess this has been one of their little hobbies for quite some time."

"But we never hear of it."

Bart shrugged.

It was snowing outside. Montana snowing. Deep and still. Deep as your ass and still snowing. Snowmobiles whined unpleasantly down the streets.

I hate them damn machines, Du Pré thought. Used to be you had to know the country and how to move through it, now any asshole can get on one of those things and chase deer to death for the fun of it. Pigs, like the rest of them, off-road vehicles, dirt bikes, little four-wheelers.

Me, I drive one when I got to, only. I hate it.

"We are not thinking about this good enough," said Du Pré. "We look for murders, we find them. What are we doing? We say, it is someone that we don't like."

"Yes," said Bart, "because the people we don't like much were killed by, in all probability, people we do like. I love this fucking job. I get five, six calls a day, long distance, people screaming at me to catch the killers. The killers of the wolves, mind you. I want to be the only Sheriff's office in the world with an unlisted telephone number."

Du Pré laughed.

"You know, I think I go see Benetsee," he said. "I have not seen the old fart, couple weeks, take him some food and wine, tobacco. Each winter I think, he go off, we not find him till the snow melt in the spring."

Bart flipped a dart at the board.

"He'll just disappear, Gabriel," said Bart. "The coyotes will eat him and then, someday, make little coyotes. One kind of immortality."

Corey Banning's big four-wheel-drive diesel pickup pulled up and they heard the door slam on the truck. She barged in, knocking the snow off her high packs, and tossed her cowboy hat at the hat tree. The hat landed precisely on a peg.

"You ain't missed yet," said Bart.

"I never miss," said Corey. "Too bad about the St. Francis brothers. We get to wait till they kill some poor whore, I guess."

"How's tricks?" said Bart.

Corey shrugged. "I am getting nothing," she said, "which I expected to get. Killing four Fish and Wildlife agents is a federal offense and so I am here forever. I may retire here. I may die here. But I do not go away from here without I get 'em *all*."

"Can't die till you get 'em," said Bart, "but I don't know, we may just never find out. You remember that guy got shot in Missouri, the thug, by the townspeople? They never found out on that one."

"They didn't send me," said Corey Banning. "You don't have to be very smart to be an FBI agent if you're a guy. President, either, for that matter. I've been north and east. Nothing there. Talked to everybody that the Sheriff's said could possibly have done it. You know what they do? They shrug. Ask them where they were that day, they shrug. Ask them is there anything they can think of to help me, they shrug. They sure ain't about to give anyone up. You'd think there'd be one greedy prick or one jealous wife or one goddamned snitch here, but they haven't bothered talking to me."

"They won't," said Bart. "They think Washington, D.C., is something that ought to be nuked and they'd just have to shoot it if it came here. And Gabriel was saying just before you flounced in that it was someone we know and like and they probably won't ever be caught. We have no evidence. Nothing. Not a slug, a fingerprint, nothing. Did your people find anything at all?"

Corey Banning shook her head.

"All the killers have to do is keep quiet," said Bart, "that's all. They don't even have to be careful. Even if there were two of them, and one confessed and turned in the other, we can't get a conviction."

"I ain't looking at it right," said Corey. "It's like tracking an animal. You don't look at the ground right, you lose 'em."

"That ground up there, under ten feet of snow," said Du Pré, "you won't find nothing. You know how to track something, you know how not to leave any. I am going to Benetsee's now, see what he say. He say that these people killed, the earth hates them, he has never known the earth hating like this before."

"I would think," said Corey, "that the earth would hate rip-off miners and such a lot more."

Du Pré shook his head.

That old man know something, or maybe doesn't yet, he is lost in his dreams, Du Pré thought.

We all are.

What is for the earth to hate, anyway? It still be here long after people have left it, all. I don't think we last much.

"Well," said Du Pré, "I go see that old fart now. I got this funny feeling that even if he know something, he won't tell us either."

Several cars went by outside, laboring through the deep snow. The plows had been through and would be again soon. The county was so sparsely populated that there were few plows. Almost everyone had a high-set four-wheel-drive truck. There was damn little north of Toussaint and Cooper but the Wolf Mountains, not much against winds that came from the North Pole.

The telephone rang. Bart had his boots up on his desk and a cup of coffee in his hand. He answered his own telephone; the dispatcher for the radio calls worked out of her house, six miles away.

Bart listened. His boots thumped down on the floor.

Du Pré waited.

"Well," said Bart, "I don't blame you, Susan, but I'd appreciate it if you didn't shoot anybody. I'll be right there."

"What?" said Corey Banning.

"Unbelievable," said Bart. "There are about a hundred flatlanders in that little park across from the bar. Several of them came into the bar and they told Susan that they were having a memorial service for the martyrs who died for the wolves. Then they say that they want to hold it inside the saloon since it's snowing outside."

Yah, thought Du Pré, I can see Susan listening to that. Hear what she say to it, too. They don't move fast enough for her, down go her hand and up come the shotgun. Oh, I hope Benny is there soon.

"I guess we had better go and see what the hell is going on," said Bart, "though I don't quite understand why they are doing this now. The murder victims have been dead for quite some time, and so have the wolves."

"I don't think these people thought much about it until someone did it for them," said Du Pré. "I think we got a bunch of extremely dumb people there, probably that asshole Bucky Dassault there, too, saying he is Benjamin Medicine Eagle, and I am worried some because maybe three hours from now this snow it stop and then it get cold and a big wind from the northwest, very cold big wind. Then maybe some more snow."

Bart looked at Du Pré.

"I think we had better get the high school set up for 'em and send for the Red Cross," he said.

"You read this weather pretty good," said Corey Banning. "According to the weather reports, that is exactly what is going to happen. And there is a hell of a snowstorm coming in fifty points north of this one. The Alberta Clipper."

Du Pré nodded. "We don't have one of them for seven years, and it was very bad."

"Christ," said Bart, "we got to get that damn highway closed down. I'll call 'em now. All three of them, I'll ask the Highway Patrol to close down."

"I better go on over there," said Du Pré, "see what is going on. That Susan, they threaten her too much she will shoot, you know."

"I'll follow," said Corey Banning.

Bart slammed the phone down.

"Goddamn it," he yelled. "Those bastards!"

"Ah?" said Du Pré.

"They've had a ton of cars headed this way and didn't do dick. They could have called me. Any car left Miles City this morning ain't gonna make it here."

"Christ," said Corey.

"I don't know," said Du Pré. "Usually them ranchers will help but this word gets round they might not."

"They'll help," said Corey Banning.

"I hope so," said Bart.

"They're our people," said Corey Banning, "of course they will. They'll save 'em and shelter 'em and feed 'em. And I bet they won't say a word to these idiots all the time they're doin' it."

Du Pré nodded, and they went out the door.

✤ CHAPTER 12 ✤

It was still pretty warm out, though the air had a crystal-line bite to it. The flakes of snow were getting smaller.

Du Pré had to park a half mile from the Toussaint Bar, clear out of town. There were stalled and stuck cars all over the road, and when he slogged into town there were cars and silly little four-wheel-drive station wagons all over the place, in people's yards, on the playground next to the little elementary school.

There was a crowd across the road from the Toussaint Bar, circling a bonfire made of the picnic tables the high school kids in Cooper had made for the tourists. Someone wearing a feathered headdress was ranting from the back of a pickup truck. Du Pré couldn't hear the words. He didn't need to.

Bucky Dassault. Child molester, alcohol and drug counselor, and then he is Benjamin Medicine Eagle, rubbing crystals and talking to fools.

What they call them? New Age?

Same old crap, con artists ripping off fools. Ah, hell, Catholic Church it start off that way. They all do. Jesus probably has three walnut shells, one dried pea, then he's dead and can't be questioned.

I maybe kick the shit of Bucky out of him, I don't think Bart care.

Du Pré tried the front door of the bar. It was locked.

He pounded on it and hollered.

In a couple minutes Benny opened it.

He had an eye swelling shut. Du Pré slipped through the door and Benny threw the bolt to.

Susan stuck her head up from behind the bar. She spat out a pink stream of water.

"Jesus," said Du Pré, "what the fuck happened?"

"Little fight," said Benny, "but we got 'em out finally. I got this and Susan got hit in the mouth, somebody threw a full can of beer they brought in."

Christ.

Someone pounded on the door. Du Pré went and opened it. Corey slid in. He locked it again.

"This is a mess comin' on pretty fast," she said. "We got

to get those damn fools over to the high school before the Alberta Clipper gets here. Got eighty-mile winds and a lot of snow. Who's the fucking Uncle Tonto giving the speech?"

"Nobody," said Du Pré. "Listen, I maybe need your help, Corey. You come with me. When I tell you, look over there a minute, then when I tell you it is all right, you can look back, then you speak to these people. We can take care of them at the high school in Cooper, but not here, we don't got the room."

"You wouldn't be thinking of punching out the lights of that idiot in the feathers over there, would you?" she said.

"Oh, no," said Du Pré. "That would be assault. Against the law. I would not do that thing."

"I'll judge what I see and I don't," said Corey Banning. "Let's go do something right for once."

They went out. The snow was packed down in the street and the little park. Du Pré walked up to Bucky Dassault, who had his back to him, jerked his feet out from under him. Bucky's knees hit the tailgate of the pickup, and then his hands.

Du Pré grabbed him by the collar and twisted him round.

"Shut up, you," said Du Pré. "I kick you half dead, you hear?"

Bucky opened his mouth.

Du Pré punched him hard, dumped him on the ground, and kicked him several times.

"Will you just do it and not enjoy yourself so much?" said Corey. "We got work to do, you know."

Du Pré nodded and he cracked Bucky on the back of the skull with his nine-millimeter.

The crowd watched silently.

Corey cupped her hands around her mouth.

"I am Special Agent Corey Banning, FBI," she said, "and

you are in great danger. There is a terrible storm coming and you need to go back down this highway immediately"—she pointed—"to the Cooper High School. There isn't room for all of you here, and you didn't impress the natives well. Please go now. You could die. Do not go any farther than Cooper. If you try to go back to Billings you will die. Go now to Cooper. We have not got much time. Help each other. Get the cars turned around and on the way. Start with the ones in the back."

The crowd stared at her.

Sheep, thought Du Pré. I have seen these faces going into a slaughterhouse. Same expressions.

"We came to honor the people killed for the wolves," shouted one tall, greasy-looking hippie in the back.

"I ain't going to argue with you," said Corey Banning. "You've done worn out your welcome here. Get going or freeze to death. There's not much room here. If women with young children get stranded there may be room for you. Maybe not. There's no time. Get going."

The crowd shifted and then it began to break up. The people moved back toward the scattered cars, and soon the furthest ones were grinding back down the road to Cooper.

A man and a woman waited till they could get through to Corey, still standing by the pickup. Bucky Dassault was still flat on his face in the snow. Groaning a little.

Damn, thought Du Pré, I wanted to maybe kill him, he was a public danger.

"Agent Banning," said the woman, "I'm from the Minneapolis *Star*. Bobbie Larkin. He's from Seattle. Reporters. Now, you are investigating these murders, and nothing has been found? At all? You have no leads? Nothing? Why is the FBI stymied? Do you expect a break in this case? Six people have been killed and not one statement has been made by you or the regional office. What's the story?"

Corey Banning tucked a packet of snoose in her cheek

and she chewed it some. She looked levelly at them and didn't say one word.

"Why did the deputy attack that man?" Bobbie Larkin went on.

"You knew him," said Du Pré. "You would maybe run over him, your car. We got a bad storm coming in and these foolish people could die in it, you know. Bucky, here, he don't care about that."

Corey Banning stepped down off the back of the truck and she walked off toward the Toussaint Bar.

"No comment?" shouted the woman reporter at Banning's back.

"You better get to Cooper," said Du Pré. "We are not kidding, it will be thirty below, three hours, then the big storm, stay cold. It is from the Arctic, not the Pacific, this storm. You will not be able to see ten feet and if you get out of your car in it you try to walk somewhere you die maybe fifty yards."

He jerked Bucky Dassault to his feet.

"You fucking prick," said Du Pré, "anybody die because you start this chicken-shit I will personally kill you very dead, I swear to you. *Anybody.* What you doing? Make a video? Sell it, these fools? I come look at your ads, such."

"I . . ." said Bucky.

Du Pré bashed him in the mouth, slammed him face-down on the bed of the pickup, and handcuffed him. He jerked him up by his hair and shoved him off to the bar.

"That's police brutality!" yelled the guy from Seattle.

Du Pré left Bucky standing.

"Listen, you stupid motherfuckers," he said, "I think lot of people die because this asshole set up this fool memorial service. Pocket all the donations, I bet. He say we have it here. He don't *care* that they die. He would never think of it. He finally think he make some money, get to screw some pretty women. He never think of it. I will be out, three, maybe four days now. All others, too. We try to save all these dumb people you know. And if they are dead, it is because of this prick, maybe some of the people come here, you know. Now he do this and I got to clean up after him. You maybe understand. This is not a lie. It is not a game. That storm she will be here soon. Anybody on the highway, they don't know how to stay alive, they are dead. You want to bet me how many, uh? I think maybe a lot. We try, but the snowdrifts, can't see so good, maybe a car in there, maybe not. And these people here, some of them maybe die trying to save people they don't like, like they didn't like the ones that got killed. Why should they?"

The reporters looked at each other.

"So I arrest him now," said Du Pré, "and I will throw his ass in jail. And when we add up the dead, you tell me I did a wrong thing."

Du Pré shoved Bucky Dassault up to the front door of the bar and he slammed Bucky's face into it.

Benny unlocked it.

"He looks kinda worn," said Benny.

Du Pré shoved him inside. He jammed him down in a chair. He pulled out his nine-millimeter and jammed it between Bucky's eyes.

"I know people will die in this," he said. "I maybe kill you now, save the time. I know people die. Some, my friends, they die, because of this I will kill you. I make you that promise."

The telephone rang. Susan Klein answered.

She listened. She waved to Du Pré.

Du Pré walked over and grabbed the phone.

"It is me," he said.

"Booger Tom just called me," said Bart, "and he said eight people took off this morning on snowshoes, headed up into the Wolfs."

67

"You got sleds for them snowmobiles in your barn?" said Du Pré.

"Four," said Bart.

"OK," said Du Pré. "I call Raymond, maybe Booger Tom, one of your cowboys."

"Jesus," said Bart.

Du Pré walked back over to Bucky.

"I think maybe you killed eight people," he said softly. "You better pray I can find them."

He nodded to Benny and Susan and Corey and he went out the door.

✤ CHAPTER 13 ✤

No," said Booger Tom, "I told him *snowmobiles*. Four of 'em. They had one sled, piled up with *snowshoes*, which they is gonna need, soon's their machines sink out of sight, couple thousand feet up."

"OK," said Du Pré, "I guess we go now. Catch them pretty quick. When our machines quit, we turn around, that's it. We can't get them out then."

We got the one hope, thought Du Pré, we are better on these than they are on theirs. They are stuck and we find them right away. This snow it is graining down. They make it to the steep slopes the noise they make bring down avalanche for sure. Hear one of them we turn around, too. They can't fly a helicopter in that narrow canyon without bringing all that snow down.

It is like they run into a burning house with it ready to come down.

But I got to go look.

Oregon license plates. That is about right.

"OK," said Du Pré to Booger Tom, Raymond, and Benny Klein. "We go on up and when we can't go farther we turn around. We don't got much time, find these people, you know, minute the snow stop, sun come out and wind come up then we got to turn around and head back right then. The snow start coming down. We go pretty far, when it gets bad I go on alone, far as I can, I call you I need you. When I got to turn round that is it."

"Du Pré," said Raymond, "I don't let you do that."

"Raymond," said Du Pré, "my girls, they are grown up. You are married to one, you got her the ten kids, you. I don't think we got time to talk."

Du Pré started his snow machine and moved off. The others followed. They went through Bart's big bench pasture, cutting off a couple of miles, and came down a side-hill trail to the Forest Service trail which ran up into the Wolfs in the Cooper Creek drainage.

There were some faint signs of passage; where trees screened the trail there were almost invisible dips in the snow's surface in lines too straight to have fallen from the sky.

Du Pré ran the machine up the trail, looking ahead to where the steep slopes narrowed in. The snow was heavy on them, poised to slide. He shot out into a meadow and saw the snow machines piled at the far end. Two of them were tangled; one must have followed too closely when the front one's skis sank and caught something.

The top of the damn barbed-wire gate, Du Pré thought. Pretty deep, this snow.

Du Pré slowed and his machine began to sink. He came to a stop by the jumbled snowmobiles.

There was a more clearly drawn trail headed up the canyon. Du Pré squinted. Couple places where someone had fallen over. Them snowshoes, he thought, they don't got throttles on them, got to know what you are doing. But they must have the long ones, little ones would just sink.

Du Pré checked the snowshoes strapped to the sled he was pulling. Six feet long with high raised front tips, Alaska trappers. He waved at the three men behind him, cranked up his machine, and pulled up slowly to the gate. He got out and stood on the front skis and he reached down in the snow till he found the wire and cut it with the dikes he had in his parka.

Temperature is dropping, sun is up there, light is rising. I don't got much time. They don't got much time.

Little spoiled brats I am trying to save. They don't let me, fuck them. I turn round, first thing they say I don't like. No, I won't. They are just plenty dumb is all.

Du Pré pulled the wire up and pushed it over. He wound the engine up and wallowed forward till the track caught on the next wire down, giving him a springboard.

Ride in, walk out, I think, he thought.

He kept the machine flat out. The rear end wallowed through the light snow; the snowmobile jumped up and down a little. Like skating on black ice. Go over it fast, fine; slow, it break.

There was a tall grove of firs at the very mouth of the narrow canyon. Canyons on the north side of the Wolfs were U-shaped, but the glaciers hadn't come down the south side. He roared out the other side onto the braided tiny plain the creek had kept from the trees. It ran high and swift in spring for a couple weeks, then sank to a trickle for the rest of the year.

Du Pré saw movement up ahead. Someone standing in the snow, waving. He pulled up to the figure and slowed and the snowmobile sank, the front end going deepest from the weight of the engine.

Du Pré clambered back to the sled and put on the snowshoes and he pumped over to the snow-covered fool waving at him, his knees lifting high to pull up the snowshoe's toes and set them again.

He stopped next to the idiot.

"Help me, help me," she said. She had a muffler wrapped round her head. Much frost where she had breathed through it. The cold air was sliding down the canyon. Blue cold.

"You, quiet," Du Pré hissed. "I get you out but we got snow above which is wanting to slide. You got snowshoes?"

She dug out a pair from the snow. She had been standing on them.

"OK," Du Pré whispered, "now I go and get the sled, pull it over, you put on these and we go back. We got to hurry, sun come out the snow it loosen."

She nodded.

Du Pré got the sled and she clambered on it and he pulled it over to the track the snowmobile had made.

He scraped the snow off her packs and got her tied to the snowshoes.

"We got to get out of here some quick," he hissed. "No noise."

She nodded.

Du Pré stomped himself around and he started down the trail.

Usually, I let them go ahead but I got to pull this one along. We got three miles, snow it come down anytime. Another avalanche go boom, jet overhead, owl he fart. We either make it or not. Probably not. I don't give us much chance.

Du Pré's ears crackled. Something talking to him. The snow.

71

I will kill you now, Du Pré, they find you in the spring, your face color of red wine.

I get out of here I kill that damn Bucky Dassault. I kill him with a shovel. I want to hear it ring.

Hard going, even in the pressed track the snow machine had made.

Too heavy to turn around, and once I slow down that is it. The snow it does not come down for that, maybe not for us.

I loosened it a lot.

There was a terrible boom behind them.

The other seven be dead under that, for sure, thought Du Pré.

He looked back. She was ten feet behind him, arms swinging, keeping up.

Breath coming hard, better slow down, I can't carry her. He stopped.

"We rest a minute," he said. "Soon as you can go we go. I keep looking back for you, I will not leave you."

She was sobbing, her breath choppy.

She nodded.

"We go," said Du Pré.

Ten more minutes, halfway there, the worst place just before we get out.

Hail Mary and you burn some sweet grass, old Benetsee. Need everybody now.

His ears were crackling more. A sound I cannot hear. What?

Du Pré glanced up. There were no trees above him on either side. The snowslides scraped them off. Seedlings survived the snow till they got big enough to have stiffer trunks and then they were snapped off. Just grass up there. And rock. Seventy-degree slopes.

Got a slick base, had sleet, it froze.

It come like sand down a tilted mirror when it come. Come hard enough, the vacuum suck our lungs out our mouths, look like we puking pink foam, red lumps in it.

Du Pré saw a great horned owl float past in front of him. Very bad sign in the daylight, that. Someone die now. Always been for me, someone die I see an owl, sunlight.

Ten more minutes. Du Pré stopped. She was thirty feet behind him, laboring, exhausted.

She struggled up to him.

Du Pré held his hand in front of her. She grabbed it.

"We got just the one mile, little less, to go," he said, "but we got to move pretty quick, more the sun up top the more the snow wants to slide down here."

She gasped and moaned.

"We go a little slower maybe," said Du Pré.

They went on.

Ears are crackling more, like I got a power cable next to them.

"Help me!" she screamed behind him.

Du Pré turned. She had fallen over, her snowshoes were up on the track, and she was down in the snow at an angle. She was flailing frantically. She screamed and screamed.

Du Pré heard the boom above, the cornices breaking off and falling hard into the stacked snow below.

A loud rush, like a train.

He stood on her snowshoes so he could find her, if he lived through the snow rushing down on them.

The wind in front of the snow wave hit him. He crouched in a ball.

The snow slammed down.

Du Pré held his hands to his face, smelled the wet leather of the mittens.

Whump.

Crushed in the dark.

✤ CHAPTER 14 ✤

Du Pré dug at his eyes. He took off his mittens and scraped the snow out of his eye pits. Drops of water ran down his cheeks. He blinked. There was a very faint light. He felt for his snowshoes. They were still there.

Only problem I got I don't know which way is up, now. If I ever know which way is up. Could be I am upside down.

Don't know how far up to the light, six inches? No, light too dim. Very dim.

No light at all.

Du Pré reached in his coat and fumbled for his cigarette lighter.

Not there.

He tried his other pocket. A book of matches.

He spent a few minutes trying to light them but his breath was melting the snow and he couldn't strike them with mittens on and they got wet and stayed that way.

OK. I got spit. Du Pré pushed some spittle out on his lip. He felt for it with a finger. Sitting on his cheek. Left cheek is down some.

He wriggled and moved in that direction, tried it again. Felt for a drop. Not there.

He spat again, softly.

The spittle landed in his palm.

Thank you, whichever god, I know where down is now.

Du Pré began to claw his way up. He shoved and packed the snow, making a chamber. He pulled his snowshoes round to where he thought they would be more or less parallel to the ground.

Another goober, my palm.

Straight down.

Well, if I am not forty feet under here I may live, you know.

But the bad storm it is coming. I hope those goddamned fools go on home before they can't get there.

They won't. My friends, they die here with me.

Du Pré reached as far as he could out and down.

He yelled.

She was not there.

He took off his left snowshoe and poked down.

Nothing.

Well, that is the owl, I guess.

All of this for nothing, I guess.

Du Pré dug and dug and pulled his snowshoes up and dug some more.

He couldn't get any higher. He had reached as high as he could. He took off his parka and set it to the side, then stepped on it with his right snowshoe. He lifted the left one and poked upward. The long trapper gave him another six feet of reach.

Light.

Now all I got to do is get to it.

He dug his hand into the snow wall beside him.

A tree. Little cottonwood.

Climb up the tree to heaven.

Like when I was little kid, there, the big spruce in the back of the house, get that pitch over me, my hair, my mother she go crazy. Your clothes! Your hands!

Du Pré shifted round till he could get his snowshoes on each side of the tree.

Not a very big tree, this.

A stub.

He struggled till he could hook his left snowshoe on it and then he slowly lifted himself. Brushed the snow away from his right snowshoe.

I need these, I get out.

Hope all the snow come down. Not just one side of the canyon.

His hands slipped off the top of the tree, where the avalanche had broken off the crown.

Du Pré shoved the snow back into the hole behind him.

He could see up. The mountainside was bare.

He struggled a long time to get perched on the broken top of the tree and then he slowly rose up.

He heard a snowmobile.

He waved. The machine turned toward him. The driver saw him.

Raymond.

Du Pré hauled himself up on the back seat. He undid the ties of the snowshoes and he pulled them off and tossed them in the sled Raymond was pulling.

"Where are Benny, Booger Tom?" said Du Pré.

"They are up the canyon. When the snow come on down it make it easier, they were to take one last ride up, look for you. You find anybody?"

"I find a woman," said Du Pré, "but she is pulled away, the snow."

Du Pré heard the other machines screaming back down the canyon toward them.

Booger Tom and Benny whined up. They cut their throttles back. The snow was tighter than it had been before the avalanche.

"We go home!" said Du Pré.

Them owl, they don't lie. We stay here, the Clipper hit, we stay here till spring.

No one could hear him. He pointed down the canyon and they nodded and took off. Du Pré threw himself at the sled and crawled in and Raymond pulled away, traveling a little faster than the others. The sled's bottom kept his track from digging in too deep.

They made their way through the gate and down to the trail up to the bench.

The clouds far off in the northwest were black and headed in fast. Silver-black, snow and cold.

The sun shone bright. It seemed warm.

It feel warm, thought Du Pré, even though it is twenty below.

Bart's house came in view, smoke rising straight up and quickly, because of the cold, cold, still air.

They roared into the compound, pulled the snowmobiles into the barn, and walked to the house.

Du Pré was suddenly freezing. He was wet from snow falling inside his clothes. He began to shiver.

Hypothermia.

He went into the house and got his clothes off, dropping them as he moved toward the master bedroom and the whirlpool bath. It was full and hot. He got in and switched on the jets.

He leaned back with his shoulders against one of the jets. Hot water played hard against his back. He stuck his feet against another.

Still shivering, little black spots danced in front of his eyes.

Booger Tom came in with a steaming pot of tea. He poured it into a big glass and handed the glass to Du Pré.

Hot whiskey toddy, lemon.

Du Pré sipped. Not too warm. He gulped it down and held out the glass again.

He leaned back.

"I thank you, my friend," he said.

"You're welcome. Glad you dug yourself out. See, I said, well, I won't leave till I find him, and then Benny said

77

he wouldn't leave if I didn't. Raymond said he'd leave, he's got all them kids. Smart, and we admire him for it. And then he wouldn't, either."

Du Pré nodded. All my grandbabies there, good, he got to take care of them. We both dead, it is tough on Jacqueline.

"Benny, Raymond, they go home?" said Du Pré.

"Yup," said Booger Tom. "You drink that, 'fore it gets cold."

Du Pré did. The hot whiskey was blooming in his belly.

They tell me, medic class, don't do this. Screw them. We get a different kind of hypothermia in the mountains.

"Did you call my Madelaine?"

"Sure," said Booger Tom. "Why a beautiful woman would want anything to do with you, you worthless son of a bitch, bumfoozles me, but she does, and I did."

The front door opened.

"Du Pré!" Madelaine yelled.

"Back here!" said Booger Tom.

Her boots thumped on the puncheon floors.

She came into the steamy bathroom.

"Ah," she said, "how you feel?"

"Some better," said Du Pré. "I start that hypothermia."

Madelaine nodded. "How many go up?"

"Eight," said Booger Tom. "Dumb shits."

"Du Pré," said Madelaine, "you don't go up there, when you know the people dead."

"I found one," said Du Pré. "Bringing her back, tell her be quiet. She fall down, she scream. Avalanche."

"You get killed I hate you for it, these fools," said Madelaine.

Du Pré nodded.

I had to go. I don't argue, me, now.

But not again.

When they got no chance.

The Alberta Clipper slammed against the house suddenly. The place shook, the wind screamed overhead.

Madelaine was praying. For all the lost souls.

Du Pré didn't have to ask her.

✤ CHAPTER 15 ✤

Du Pré," said Madelaine, "we are just going to run out
of food here, you know, I hope they get that damn
road open."

"It is open," said Du Pré. "Bart just got the word.
Plowed. No more snow. So they go now."

The pilgrims had been stuck in the Cooper High School
gym all week. The local people had done what they could
to feed them and make them comfortable. One end of the
basketball court was a big soup kitchen, and they had rolled
out the wrestling mats. The place stank.

"That damn Bucky Dassault," said Du Pré. "I find
him . . ."

"It is not him," said Madelaine. "You have not been in
the gym. It is four, five people live in that Jackson Hole
come here, sent out all these flyers, do this. I don't know
what is the big deal. Plenty wolves up in Alaska, Canada."

Du Pré shook his head.

Who these people? Some reason, them politician say
yes, here we are. Got fourteen dead people. They more or
less murder themselves. Like me, come home, find some
tourist in my house, feet up, drinking my whiskey, saying I
beat my dog, starve my horses.

Du Pré was hollow-eyed and ready to fall over. No one

had slept much, searching the roadsides for buried vehicles. One six-year-old kid he decide, my appendix needs to infect, Benny has to cut it out while a doctor in Billings talks to him. Worked out pretty good.

"I will go see about my horses," said Du Pré. "Glad I sold all them cows, I would have a couple ten ton of dead ones to bury, March."

And Benetsee. He will be all right.

The telephone rang. Madelaine picked it up, motioned to Du Pré.

"That Bart," she said. She was mad at Bart for some reason.

"Yo," said Du Pré.

"They're going," said Bart, "moving out pretty fast. Course us folk who live here want 'em gone, couple of the plow drivers got pretty good at scraping just enough off the cars parked by the road to total 'em and leave 'em drivable.

"Which is not why I called," he went on. "I arrested four of these little assholes for public endangerment and threw their little butts in jail. Guy I know in Billings called, said the TV people and the journalists are ten deep waiting to leave and come here. I told him to tell them we are wholly swamped and we can't provide lodging or food for 'em. So some of them are chartering helicopters to fly 'em back and forth. Big story, murders, now this. They're going to be after you because of the lost dumb bastards up Cooper Creek."

"Foote is here, yes?"

"Foote is here in two hours or so, yes," said Bart.

"Well," said Du Pré, "I will just send them to him, not talk to them. Pretty pushy people, them."

"I knew that," said Bart. "What I want you to do is come here pretty quick and chew these little assholes up real good. They're sitting in the cells singing 'We Shall

80

Overcome,' for Chrissakes. The prisoners' lockers are full of designer expedition gear."

"OK," said Du Pré. "I want to see about Benetsee, my horses."

"Booger Tom went over and your horses are fine," said Bart, "but I don't know about Benetsee."

"East, how the storm?" said Du Pré.

"Terrible," said Bart. "Worst one in history, if you think history is what people write down. Finally went out to sea after pasting the South. Funny thing is, they don't know where it came from. No warning, no blip on the spy satellites. Out of the Arctic and away we go."

"Yah," said Du Pré. "Well, I will go see about that old fart, then I come see those people. They sure are funny people down there on the flat. Think no one lives here or if we do we don't know how. How many people out there under the snow, huh, Bart? Missing persons? Calls they come in when?"

"Already coming in," said Bart. "Parents. Break your heart. My kid hasn't come back, my environmentalist kid. Earth First! Stone tools and raw hides. Course, they got no idea how tough it is to live off what you can *shoot*, let alone run down with a club."

"Well," said Du Pré, "that mob, gets to Miles City, Billings, they call home some."

"Not all of them," said Bart, softly. He hung up.

"Here," said Madelaine. She held out a big wad of blankets. "Got a hot meal in there. Jug of that wine he like is by the door."

Du Pré shrugged into his coat, pulled on his packs, went out, and started the Rover. He came back in and smoked while the car warmed up. Madelaine's kids were watching television. The oldest boy was in the army, and the next one down would go to the navy in June.

This time, it go faster and faster, Du Pré thought, I wonder how fast it go for old Benetsee? Faster till you are dead? Run so fast you are in the dark before you know it?

Madelaine bent over to kiss him.

"I get anything for you?" said Du Pré.

"Well," said Madelaine, "we need groceries but it will be some time we can go buy them."

"I got some, my place," said Du Pré.

"No, you don't," said Madelaine. "You don't got a can, creamed corn, I go out there while you poking in snow-drifts."

Du Pré nodded.

"Maybe I bring Benetsee, few days," he said.

"Benetsee is welcome all the time," said Madelaine, "you know that. I am some worried, old man like that, out there."

"I go by yesterday he got smoke coming out his chimney," said Du Pré.

Madelaine kissed him again. Du Pré went out to his Rover and got in and drove off. It was very cold and the snow gave good traction.

The road up to Benetsee's had been plowed but the wind had drifted the snow back in many places and Du Pré got up to fifty and bashed through the drifts.

Hope that there is not a car in one of these, he thought. Well, the plows made it through OK, hope someone's gas line did not freeze, car sitting here after the plows come through.

How many hundreds of people this storm kill? Still digging out, Alberta, Saskatchewan, east of here. Snow fall where it never did fall before.

Du Pré saw the trees that huddled close around Benetsee's cabin. Smoke rose straight up to the white-blue sky.

There was a place big enough to park in, chewed out of the drifts by the plows. Du Pré crunched over to the path between the trees. He stopped, startled.

The path was clean and so was the ground around Benet-see's little shack. It looked like a tornado had set down, swirled the snow up into drifts, and moved on. A very gentle tornado.

Du Pré walked up to the porch and Benetsee opened the door and grinned at him.

"You are alive," said Du Pré.

Benetsee nodded.

"OK," said Du Pré, "I get your things Madelaine send for you."

The old man's old dogs looked out on either side of Benetsee's knees.

Du Pré sat next to the stove while the old man drank some wine and smoked. He ate hungrily all the good food that Madelaine had sent.

Like a coyote, thought Du Pré, he eat a whole lot and then he don't need to eat a long time.

"You worried me, going to look for those fools," said Benetsee. "They thought that they could do something very smart but them mountain eat them. Hee."

"Yah," said Du Pré. "Well, I had to try there, you know. It is my job, now."

Benetsee nodded.

Du Pré started to ask about the snow and the wind around his cabin but he stopped himself. The old man would just tease him with some damn riddle. Oh, I dance, he would say. Know how, dance.

"What you going to do, them reporter come here, ask you questions?" said Du Pré. "Turn into a raven, fly away?"

"Oh, they will not bother me," said Benetsee. "I disappear."

Du Pré had seen the old man disappear many times. In rooms, people in them, no quick way out, poof, he was gone.

"I got to go, talk to those assholes set this thing up," said Du Pré. "Killed a bunch of people. That fucking Bucky Dassault I think have something to do with it."

Benetsee nodded. He drank another big glass of wine.

"He is not smart enough, be bad," said Benetsee. "Pretty dangerous. Well, I go talk to those fools, the jail."

Du Pré nodded.

Benetsee belched.

"One glass wine," the old man said, "and we go."

✤ C H A P T E R   1 6 ✤

A h," said Deputy Lawyer Foote, "I just finished chewing their asses off—my, how I talk in the sagebrush—and now I suspect Benetsee will do the same."

"Hee," said Benetsee.

"The old man gets done with them I'll let 'em go," said Bart. "I was appalled to find out that you cannot arrest people on suspicion of being stupid assholes. Lucky for Congress, ain't it?"

Booger Tom was sitting in Bart's chair, drinking coffee. The smell of whiskey got stronger the closer you got to Booger Tom's cup.

Du Pré and Benetsee followed Bart back to the cells. They were old and primitive and cold. The five people in the holding cell were all shivering in orange jail jumpsuits. Two men, three women.

Benetsee dragged a chair over to the cell and he sat down. He held his hand up for a smoke. Du Pré rolled him one, lit it, and stuck it in Benetsee's old brown fingers.

Benetsee smoked and he stared unblinking at the people in the cell. They began to stir and shift like a bunch of horses when the wrangler comes to cut one out.

Benetsee stared.

They could not look him in the eye.

"Why you come here?" said Benetsee, suddenly.

No answer.

"You maybe ask Bart for a red bag?" said Benetsee, turning to Du Pré. "Not a big one, maybe some flat, about this big." He gestured with his hands.

Du Pré shrugged and went on out.

Bart listened and he dug around in the locker and found the red bag, about the size of a long briefcase, very thin, made of nylon cloth. Du Pré carried it back to Benetsee.

Benetsee held it on his lap. He unzipped it. The people in the cell stirred uncomfortably. Benetsee pulled out an eagle's wing, bald eagle. He held it up, looking at the feathers.

"I keep this," said Benetsee, "it only cause you trouble. You think you can make magic? Hah. You, you maybe make coffee, boiled eggs."

Du Pré laughed.

"You come here with bad hearts," said Benetsee, "and you get a lot of people killed, one way, another. Very foolish. You don't kill them with your hands, you kill them with your foolish talk."

The people in the cell looked at each other.

"You go home maybe," said Benetsee. "You don't come back here. Not ever. This place eat you if you do."

The old man stood. He looked levelly at the people cowering in the cell. Benetsee tucked the eagle wing under his arm and he walked back out into the room.

"Fools," he said to Bart. Bart nodded.

"I go, Toussaint now." Du Pré put his coat on.

They drove out of Cooper, down the white road. There

were still some cars shoved off to the side, their engines frozen. Du Pré parked in front of the Toussaint Bar and they went in.

Susan Klein was serving several couples lunch, rushing about. Du Pré and Benetsee sat and waited on stools at the bar.

"You need lunch?" said Susan, when she got back behind the bar. "I'm serving mooseburgers. All we had left. Illegal as hell, but hungry is hungry."

"Sure," said Du Pré.

Susan poured Du Pré some whiskey, pale yellow, a local product.

She gave Benetsee a big glass of wine.

"You can drink all the damn wine you want," said Susan to Benetsee. "But you're going to have to eat. All free."

Benetsee grinned, his few old worn brown teeth like chips of walnut.

Bill Stemple got up from his table and came over to Du Pré. He was picking his teeth. He fished in his pocket and took out a cigarette and lit it.

"Ain't this some shit," he said. "We lost some more cows, they had their damn mouths freeze shut while me and my hands were going up and down the road to find the little fuckers. Found six. Had to keep 'em in my house and feed 'em."

"Yah," said Du Pré, "well, it was plenty quiet here, long time, now we got all this fuss. But maybe it teach somebody something, I don't know."

Stemple shrugged.

"That damn FBI woman, Banning," he said, "hell, she's all over everybody, asking the same damn questions over and over. I understand that she's got to, but, Jesus, no one's gonna walk forward and say 'I did it' and nobody else knows anything. We wasn't even *here*."

Du Pré shrugged. "Soon, we going to have another

bunch of newspeople," he said. "They are coming, see the disaster. Probably say, did someone take those people, kill them, bury them under the snow?"

"I got work to do," said Stemple.

"We all got work to do," said Du Pré. "You keep your gates closed and don't shoot any of them. I do not like to arrest you."

Corey Banning slid in the door and shoved it to. She had a dark red muffler wrapped around her head. A sheepskin coat. She unwrapped the muffler. She wore a pissed-off expression.

"Christ," she said, "it ain't one thing it's another."

She stalked up to the bar and Susan poured her a double brandy.

"They're sending me some more agents," she said, "in the middle of the fucking winter. They'll freeze and get lost and die and such."

"Um," said Du Pré. "Do you care, them?"

"As much mother instinct as I got," she said, "I hate to see it. You know, frostbite. Crippled for life. They'll all be from Florida, I just know it. Christ."

She sipped her brandy.

"We got a big bunch, press coming," said Du Pré.

"Hah," she said. "That guy Foote is a plenty smart guy, there. He's got this one-page press release which says not one fucking thing in the most elegant English. Me, I just got no comment. We'll starve 'em out."

"Yah," said Du Pré. "Well, one more bad storm like this, it will not melt till June, you know. Maybe people be out there, frozen, till then."

"The bottom canyons in the Wolfs'll be eighty feet deep in snow," she said. "It may not melt down before the summer after."

Banning shrugged out of her coat. She was wearing simple ranch clothes and a stainless-steel nine-millimeter and cop holsters on her belt, handcuffs, pepper spray. She walked over to Benetsee and she put her arms around him and hugged him. She put her head down on his back.

"You know," she said softly. "You don't want to tell me and you won't and I can't make you. But you know it all, don't you. And there's not really anything that you want, so you can't be bought, and you're too old to care about anything much except praying."

Benetsee reached back and he patted her hair. He patted the stool beside him.

"You come sit here, my daughter," he said. "I will tell you what I know to tell you."

She got up on the stool and put one elbow on the bar top and she leaned her ear close to his old lips.

Benetsee whispered.

She nodded.

She listened and listened.

The other people in the bar paid and left. Du Pré went to the poker machine and lost money in it. Dumb machine, electronic.

He had a pocketful of quarters and it took him some time.

When he turned around Benetsee was gone, and Corey Banning had turned round and was looking off into the distance.

Du Pré walked over to the bar. He got another whiskey and he sat beside the FBI agent.

"Old Benetsee he just see the riddles most times," said Du Pré. "I would not get mad with him."

"Even the fucking riddles would help," said Banning.

"Sometime," said Du Pré, "you get one of them things, you know, it seems like you can untie it but you can't. You know, my father Catfoot he kill Bart's brother and we take a long time to figure it out, many years later. We never could have, but for a coyote Benetsee sent me."

Banning nodded.

"Fourteen people dead is a lot of people dead, and who-ever killed 'em is very smart," said Banning, "and there's more'n one of 'em."

Du Pré nodded.

"I know," he said, "that is a bad thing, they should not have done that."

"Lot of pressure on us," said Banning. "I may get shoved out, you know."

Du Pré nodded.

"Yah," he said, "then they send someone in who make evidence up, convict anybody, guilty, not, they don't care."

"Yeah, well, shit happens," said Corey Banning.

She sipped her brandy.

"I don't give a shit about the eight suicides under the avalanche," said Corey Banning. "I got my plateful."

✤ CHAPTER 17 ✤

The TV crews came in big motor homes with satellite dishes on the roofs. The print journalists came in rented cars and they looked for motel rooms.

Finally someone rented them a run-down house on a back street in Cooper. The place leaked water through the roof every time the heat came on and melted the snow above. The attic was full of raccoons. Raccoon shit. Nests. And they liked it there.

They shoved cameras in Du Pré's face, and they asked him questions about the dead under the avalanche. Du Pré shrugged. And he walked past them.

He was getting into his Rover outside the Toussaint Bar when a fat sleazy woman offered him several packets of hundred-dollar bills for an "exclusive" story for one of the cheap magazines sold in checkout lines at grocery stores.

Du Pré shrugged and got into his Rover and he drove off with a few reporters in pursuit. He went up the back roads, pounded and now drifted, and left them stuck there.

Du Pré stopped high up on the benchlands and he looked down on the bleak white land below, marked a little, a house here, barn, one or two rocky outcrops, the rest white on white on white.

The sun in the east high up had sun dogs on each side.

Very bad sign, that, three suns ride the sky. My people, long time since, it was colder then, I was told, pile the good buffalo robes in the lodge, get in the little hot-burning alder sticks for cooking, everyone live under the robes till the cold pass, eat a lot of pemmican, meat, fat, and berries.

You got to wait for this country, sure. This country, you be like the water, it is cold, you go to sleep till the sun comes back, then you can move through it, animals, too. Live under the snow where it is warm.

Them big white owls come down, times like this, hunt animals under the snow. Owls sit, wait, got ears so good they hear mouse under the snow, owl plunge into the snowdrift and grab that mouse.

But you got to let this country tell you what to do.

You try to tell it, it will kill you plenty quick now.

Yes.

Them people who got shot, they think these ranchers are not part of this country. They say, you are to move right on. Take your dead grandparents with you, dig them up and haul them away, we want to play here.

It is more than they cut a fence, shoot a cow maybe. That is dumb kid stuff.

But these ranchers are not so dumb, though maybe they cannot say why this make them so angry they just kill them.

Always, this country, more people come and say to the people who were here, you go away and starve, this is ours now, we want it, we are right and you are wrong.

The wind was rising up and a ground blizzard started. Du Pré put the Rover in gear and drove back down while he could still see the road, sort of. He went by another route, so he wouldn't have to help stuck reporters out of drifts and so forth.

There were several cars outside the Toussaint Bar, Benny's four-wheel Sheriff's rig, the usual battered ranch pickups.

Du Pré parked and walked up to the front door. When he put his hand on the door pull he happened to look down and there was a badly broken television camera, half sunk in the snow.

It took Du Pré a couple of minutes to see in the dim bar. The light outside was bright even through the high white haze.

Remember that time I got myself snow-blind, spent three days couldn't see and a month feeling like hot sand packed around my eyeballs.

Madelaine came over to him. He recognized her foot-steps. Broke an ankle as a little girl, made her left foot a little bit stitchy, pull the sole just some there.

"Hey, Du Pré," said Madelaine, "you don't remember me, eh?"

"Can't see you," said Du Pré. "You live here, maybe?"

"You die here you don't think pretty quick, now," said

91

Madelaine. "Say something funny quick, it is how you guys survive so long. You make us laugh we don't tear your plums off, shove them down your throat, eh?"

"Interesting times," said Susan Klein, washing the bar top. "That's an old Chinese curse. May you live in interesting times. These damn journalists are all over, blocking the doorways. Or they were till Ol' Jim found them between him and his afternoon smile."

Old Jim was in his seventies, still ranching, still breaking horses clamped down in an old bear-trap saddle. He was sitting off in a corner with a big glass of whiskey. He called a glass of whiskey a smile.

"Ill-mannered bastards shoved a microphone in my face and wouldn't get out of the damn way," boomed Old Jim, "so I cracked a couple of their heads together. Christ, it used to be quiet round here."

Du Pré laughed.

One of the newspaper reporters came out of the men's room and he saw Du Pré and edged toward him.

"Not in here, you," snapped Susan. "You got a question for Gabriel, you find him someplace else. I have absolutely had it with you people bothering my customers."

The man slunk toward the door.

"They'll be gone soon," said Susan, ignoring the journalist. "No story here, I guess, until the snow melts enough to find those poor fools up Cooper's Canyon. Almost got one out, didn't you?"

The reporter had stopped.

"Shit," said Susan.

Du Pré shrugged. He tapped the bar top and Susan poured him a whiskey.

Old Jim and Susan and Du Pré and Madelaine stared at the man till he gave up and left.

"Good thing this all didn't happen in the summer," said Old Jim. "As it is the bastards get frozen pretty quick and then they go away."

They will be back, though, Du Pré thought, they will be back.

"We are at Jacqueline's and Raymond's for dinner," said Madelaine. "Couple hours. My kids are liking cook for themselves, when I am gone they can use the phone all the time."

Du Pré sat thinking, while Madelaine and Susan chatted. He drank whiskey. Old Jim joined them. Benny arrived, then Bart and Booger Tom and Packy and his wife and several other townsfolk.

Deputy Lawyer Foote came.

"The journalists are pulling out," he said. "They starve rather quickly."

Du Pré grunted.

Bart stacked wood in the big old stone fireplace at the far end of the barroom. He lit the fire and stood back and poked at it till the flames caught well.

It was growing dark, fast. The shortest days of the year were on them. Christmas. A new year after.

Du Pré got his fiddle from his Rover and he let it warm for a few minutes and then he tuned it and he played some slow tunes, laments, the songs of the voyageurs on sleepless nights when they were homesick and lonely for their families and women, all the things there were not in the endless black-green forests of the North.

Bales of furs.

Carry them for the Hudson's Bay Company. Sucking the furs out of all Canada, pulling them in with trade guns and rum, blankets and beads, axes and hatchets and knives and brass kettles. Priests pull the souls along into heaven.

If that was real.

But the Hudson's Bay Company was. HBC. Here Before Christ.

On them old-time long voyage, take a whole year, sometimes two, while the women raise babies and make the canoes. Make them good and tight and strong so their men don't drown.

Du Pré thought of the dark he had been buried alive in, holding himself hard to the light, reaching up through the snow above him to heaven, shining through the hem of the storm come down from the North where hell really is, it is cold.

Dark forests. Ice. Sun dogs. Big land waiting and hungry.

Du Pré played his heart. Up out of the ice, the dark ice.

Eight people under the avalanche, frozen faces turning dark red, long frost crystals growing out of their eyes. Maybe even some still alive, yes, it could be. Nothing to be done.

How many voyageurs end up in the bellies of wolves and coyotes, badgers and skunks and magpies and ravens?

Play for them.

Play for everybody ever died in the cold.

I will rot in the earth but the music is forever, God breathes it in and out.

Du Pré let the last note die.

He reached out for the whiskey in front of him.

He drank. He looked over at his friends and his lover.

They were staring at him.

Corey Banning had come in while he was playing.

Tears ran down her cheeks.

"It is time we go to dinner," said Madelaine. "You come now."

Du Pré nodded, and finished his whiskey, and packed his fiddle away.

✤ CHAPTER 18 ✤

Right after New Year's an arctic air mass lumbered down the front of the Rockies. The mass was huge and very cold. It stretched from Montana to Minnesota. Some nights, the temperature fell to fifty-five degrees below zero. Water pipes burst. Smoke from chimneys rose straight up in yellow-white columns.

Du Pré walked out behind his house one glittering morning, looked up at the white sky, and shook his head. He glanced at the outbuildings and a wispy plume of steam caught his eye. It was coming from a crack in the siding of the barn.

He went back in the house and got a shotgun and shoved some rounds of buckshot into the magazine, racked one home.

Bear in my damn barn.

He went in cautiously. He gauged where the plume of breath had come from outside against the dark shadowed walls. The bear had crawled under some bales of straw and broken the ties. Fluffed the straw up for a bed and comforter.

Du Pré stood a few feet from the animal. He heard gentle snoring.

He shrugged.

Me, I wish that I could sleep till it gets warmer. When it gets warmer, out you go. Not now.

He had his Rover plugged in to an electrical outlet, so the

engine was warm, but when he started the engine the belts shrieked piercingly for fifteen minutes before friction warmed them enough to grab properly. When he drove off, the flat spots where the tires had set against the ground thumped loudly.

He'd left little trickles of water running from the taps.

If them cast-iron drainpipes freeze up I'll have fun, he thought, as he drove slowly down the snow-packed county road. *Thump THUMP thwap THUMP.* The paved highway was pretty clear when he got to it, but the tires were still out of round and didn't warm up enough to pop back to their intended shape until just before he turned off into Toussaint.

Benny Klein had tacked a temporary airlock out in front of the bar, a sloppy arrangement of plastic and scraps of lath, to cut down on the blasts of arctic air that burst into the saloon every time the door opened. Du Pré pushed through the hanging sheets and he rearranged them; they were tattered and breaking from the cold. He opened the door quickly and slammed it shut. A pane of glass in one of the front windows went pop!

"Little more respect for my property there, Gabriel," said Susan Klein. She came out from behind the bar with a roll of wide clear tape. Several other panes were patched.

"When we last have this?" said Du Pré. "Maybe '89? Yeah, three weeks it was fifty below every night. Old man Thompson froze to death, went out to check his stock, slipped and broke his hip."

"Yeah," said Susan. "Benny went out to check on him that afternoon, but he was dead. Benny's still sad over it, felt he should have gone that morning, but old man Thompson, he didn't like being hovered over, remember, he'd about run Benny off the day before."

"You see that Bart?"

"He called a little bit ago, looking for you. Said he'd be

96

in for lunch. I told him we were having iceworm salad."

"Nobody doing ver' much right now," Du Pré said. He thought of the FBIs in the trailer, all the pipes frozen— spraying water had hit a fuse box and blown all the neutral wires out, and then the cold had pulled the aluminum skin away from the frame, so the next good wind would shuck the hide off the roof.

Couldn't happen to a nicer bunch of folks, Du Pré thought sourly. But I like that Corey Banning. She is pret' edgy these days, like a hawk don't got anything moving down on the land below. Nothing to do.

Susan Klein shoved a bottle of whiskey across the bar top and a short glass.

"The ice machine froze up," she said. "If you require ice, you may just hump your stumps outside there, where you will find all you need."

Du Pré laughed.

"Anything happens to satellite TV," said Susan, "the murder rate here'll look like Miami's the first night. By eleven P.M. Gives us a little idea what it was like here a hundred years ago, people going insane."

Du Pré poured himself a whiskey. He rolled a cigarette and lit it and he looked at the smoke rising to the ceiling.

Oh, yes, them winter, maybe 1910, when that Black Jack Pershing he come and round up the Métis and shove them in cattle cars, it is forty below, and he send couple of thousand of us, North Dakota, to Pembina, throw us off.

Don't take us here, we are citizens, take the poor Métis from Great Falls, Helena, Lewiston, they don't know what country they are in. How many die that time? Four hundred, I think my grand-père say, they froze in the boxcars, they starve in North Dakota, under the three suns in the sky, them sun dogs.

People. Damn. All them honyockers Jim Hill sucker into homesteads, little farms on the plains, whole families found frozen round the stoves in the spring. Starved to death. Some live, there are raving crazy people screaming in the spring mud, everybody that knew who they were has died. Coyotes, they eat the dead in the houses. Here, the Dakotas, down to Nebraska, they say there are twenty thousand poor farmers and their families die that winter.

This damn winter, when it is like this it scares my bones.

My blood, it remembers the taste of boiled moccasins, worse things that my people ate.

Got no songs about that. 'Less you count the burial hymns, the church. So cold, the fiddles, they broke.

The door banged open and Bart and Corey Banning came in, their faces red from the short dash from car to warmth. Bart shoved the door to and they both stamped their feet, in their heavy felt-lined packs.

The saloon was hot. Benny had put a second woodstove in, near the door, and both of them were roaring. But if you went near the walls the cold reached out. The single-paned windows had sketches of frost in their corners.

Corey and Bart shucked off their down parkas and vests. They came over to Du Pré.

"What's shaking'?" said Corey.

"Um," said Du Pré, "I got a bear in my barn, he is sleeping, I did not have the heart to run him out."

"What kind of bear?" said Bart.

"Sleepy one," said Du Pré. "He is under the straw there, but he is not big, his tracks are maybe a two-year bear's."

"I love this weather," said Corey Banning. "My superiors are sitting on their big fat warm asses in Washington, wondering why I ain't run all these foul perpetrators to earth. Two of the Butte office's turkeys went off to nail some poor schmo on a warrant, car stalled, they walked for a ways, and they are both in the hospital, not too bad, one lost four toes and the other the tips of some fingers. Oh, yeah, when they got cold, they ran like hell. *Bright guys.*

Frostbit some of their lungs, got necrosis pneumonia."

"Ol' Corey here's always pleased to hear her fellow agents have about died," said Bart. "Always perks her up. Got such sympathy for 'em."

"Wussies," said Corey, "the lot of 'em."

"You going to the party?" said Bart.

Du Pré nodded.

"Party?" said Corey.

"Every January, Martins, they give a big party, cheer everybody up, they got this huge paddock they use to train horses, they build a square dance floor, barbecue couple of steers, bring in some good musicians. Everybody is invited, unless they are in jail," said Du Pré. "You should come, dance some, it will make you kinder, maybe."

Corey looked at Du Pré for a moment.

"I'll do just that," she said.

"You seen old Benetsee?" said Bart.

Du Pré shrugged. He'd been by, but the old man was gone and so were his dogs. Or the dogs had frozen to death and the old man was out under the snow somewhere.

"He is probably Club Med, some island in the Caribbean," said Du Pré. "He don't send postcards. No, I check his house and he has not been there. You know him, he comes, goes, who knows?"

"How long you know the Martins?" said Corey.

"All my life," said Du Pré. "They have that ranch, I think it is as big as Rhode Island, I read. I go there, when they ship, never any trouble."

"Never any trouble," said Corey. "I checked with Booger Tom, he worked on their ranch a while, he likes them. Booger Tom don't like anybody much."

Du Pré shrugged. He didn't know the Martins well. No one did. They kept to themselves other than the ordinary business of being good neighbors. They sent all their children east to private schools.

"There's Taylor," said Corey. "War hero, helicopter pilot, rodeo cowboy, and he's also a veterinarian. Enough to do on the ranch, he doesn't have a practice. Then there's his kid brother, Clark, West Point and he made Nam a little later. There was a third brother."

"Hall," said Du Pré. "He died pret' young, flew a plane up a box canyon and got trapped, couldn't fly out. He was only maybe nineteen."

"I like to dance," said Corey Banning.

Du Pré nodded and sipped some more whiskey.

✦ CHAPTER 19 ✦

Bootheels thumped on the hollow wooden floor. The Western swing band had been flown up from New Mexico and they were superb. All the musicians were dressed in Flash Western, expensive custom clothing heavy with embroidery.

"Bet all their boots got chipmunks fucking butterflies on 'em," said Booger Tom.

Du Pré laughed. The three hundred or so people on the dance floor were two-stepping fast. They were merry with drink and the bright music.

"Good band," said Du Pré.

Booger Tom snorted.

Bart was standing in his uniform, fully belted, over near one of the huge double-drum woodstoves. Corey Banning stood with him, in a leather jacket long enough to cover her gun.

Clark Martin, tall and dark blond, was teaching one of

his little girls to dance. The child stood on the tops of his boots and she laughed and bounced as Clark shuffled.

There were huge trestle tables against one wall of the arena, piled with food. The far corner of the building had a new false-front saloon built in it; the raw wood oozed sap and gave off a thick scent of pine. Five barkeeps shoved drinks across the bar top.

"They put on a good party," said Du Pré. He turned around and saw Booger Tom sliding around the milling couples, on his way to the bar again.

That old goat can drink some, Du Pré thought, especially when it's free.

A few people, too old to dance or too drunk, were scattered in a mass of smaller tables to the side of the bandstand. The Martin family had their own. The elder Mrs. Martin sat at it, her son Taylor next to her. She wore a purple silk blouse and a beaded vest, and she had a choker of emeralds and diamonds at her throat. White-haired and pale-skinned, fingers glittering with rings, she sat slender and erect, smiling faintly when someone would stop and say something.

Her husband die about five years ago, Du Pré thought. She looks like the queen of a small country. Small, tasteful country, lots of traditions.

Taylor was laughing a lot. He got up and took glasses in his hands and he headed off toward the bar. His mother stared straight at the dancers on the floor. She tapped with the band's rhythms, her red nails against a white saucer.

"The Queen Bee there," said Corey Banning, at Du Pré's side. Du Pré turned. "Where's Madelaine?"

"She has a kid got an ear infection," said Du Pré.

"She thinks rich folks are silly, more like," said Corey. "So do I, but I got to snoop. I'd never seen the Queen Bee—I didn't have a good enough reason to request an audience. If I got one, I'd get nothing, maybe a nice glass of sherry, some petit-fours, an offer to help me. Jesus, the old broad's moral force about blows my dandruff off, here to there. You know her?''

Du Pré shook his head. Me, I am just the nice cattle-brand inspector comes to sign off on three million dollars' worth of cows when they ship. You want to buy a thousand head of yearlings, ask if they got 'em, they nod and pause, then ask, you want them all one color? What color?

Taylor Martin returned to the table and he set down the drinks he was carrying and he looked over at Du Pré and Corey Banning and he waved generously at them to come over.

"The prince bids us come," said Corey. "Now, don't pick your nose and you can't fart within a hundred yards of the Presence, there. Come along, Du Pré, remember to genuflect when I do."

They made their way to the table. Mrs. Martin rose to greet them. When Du Pré shook her hand, it startled him. Her horsewoman's strength gripped him hard.

"Are you finding enough to eat and drink?" said Mrs. Martin. She had soft southern notes in her voice, and deep education.

"A surfeit," said Corey Banning. "What the hell do you do with this place between shindigs? Train cavalry troops?"

"Just horses," said Mrs. Martin. "The long winters are hard to bear. At least with this place, one can work. Helps me to make it through."

"Morgan and her horses are something of a family joke," said Taylor. "If my father hadn't employed cooks, her children would have starved to death."

"I had the children," said Mrs. Martin, "and that was, I think, something of a contribution. Diapers, bottles, and the daily feedings, I said, would be up to someone else. Anyone else."

Corey laughed. Du Pré smiled.

She laughs at herself, Du Pré thought. This Mrs. Martin, there is a good deal here.

"You want to talk to me, dear," said Mrs. Martin to Corey, "so let's us just go do that. Taylor, could you have some brandy sent to the greenhouse?" She lifted a suede jacket from the bench and hung it over her shoulders. She took Corey's elbow and steered her toward a door at the far end of the paddock.

"We are well out of what's next," said Taylor Martin. "Come on, I need to dispatch the brandy, and we can have a drink."

They walked over to the bar, and Taylor spoke with one of the barkeeps. The man nodded and grabbed a bottle of brandy from below the bar and he set it on a tray and put two snifters on it and filled them halfway with boiling water.

"Corey, she is kind of frustrated," said Du Pré. "It is kind of your mother to talk with her."

"Very funny," drawled Taylor Martin, "since the two of them will be sticking skewers in each other and never a hint of pain. Banning's been following very faint tracks. They don't stop here, mind you, but she naturally wonders just what goes on in our little kingdom here."

Du Pré shrugged.

If it is you people, he thought, you will come out of here and do it again, anyway. All I can do is wait.

Taylor handed Du Pré a drink. Du Pré glanced down at the man's hand. There was livid scar tissue on the back and the fingers were twisted. One of the fingers was missing, and the two joints of the little finger were gone.

"Mortar round," said Martin, holding up his hand. "I'll not forget that day. You in Nam, Du Pré?"

Du Pré shook his head. "Germany," he said. "Drank a lot of beer."

Martin nodded.

He glanced up and his jaw tightened and Du Pré turned and looked. There was a little knot of men at one corner of the dance floor starting to fight.

Martin set his drink down and moved toward them, gliding across the floor, the floating dance of a fighter closing in. Du Pré followed him. The men were yelling by now and a couple had squared off while the others backed away.

"Not here," said Taylor Martin sharply.

Young cowboys, all set for their Saturday night sport. Du Pré didn't know who they were. Maybe hands from a neighboring ranch.

The two ignored him and one balanced back to throw a punch.

Martin stepped between them and the cowboy swung. Martin reached out idly with his damaged hand and he grabbed the cowboy's wrist and twisted and then half idly swung his right bootheel into the man's kneecap. The cowboy yelped and went down.

"None of that here," said Taylor Martin, "and not outside, either. It's too cold. Now, come on, let's all go get a drink." He reached down and grabbed the fallen cowboy's shoulder and lifted him easily to his feet. The cowboy looked dumbly at Taylor.

"Damp it down or I'll break your fucking neck," said Martin.

"OK OK sorry," said the cowboy, both hands on his knee. "We just forgot ourselves, you know how it is."

Martin led the cowboys over to the bar. He told a funny story or two, saw to their drinks, and then he clapped a hand on Du Pré's shoulder and steered him away.

"Youth is very young," said Martin. "If one starts, they all do. The happy cowboy idiocy of fistfights for the fun of it."

Du Pré nodded. He'd been in a lot of them himself.

The band took a break, the fiddle and steel guitar rippling behind the lead singer's smooth and practiced voice. Talk erupted on the dance floor and knots of people headed for the bar.

"Taylor!" a voice yelled. It was Clark Martin, grinning and striding toward them.

"Saw you break the fight up," said Clark. "One of those boys works for us, you know."

Taylor nodded. "Well," he said, "till he knocks my block off he still works for us. Can't blame a man for wanting to fight a little on a Saturday night, especially with a winter as long and mean as this."

"Where's Morgan?" said Clark.

"Took that lady FBI agent to the greenhouse," said Taylor.

"Investigate the orchids?" laughed Clark.

"Place is plumb full of exotic blooms," said Taylor, "so let's get us a drink."

Du Pré couldn't help but agree.

♣ CHAPTER 20 ♣

A March blizzard lashed hard at the land. The huge flakes shot along, pushed by winds that screamed overhead. It was fairly warm, but impossible to see fifty feet.

Corey Banning and Du Pré stood at the bar. Corey was rolling a cigarette, one practiced seamless motion. She licked the paper and flipped the smoke into her lips and lit it and tapped the lighter on the scarred wood.

"Darts," she said. "This place needs a nice dartboard."

"Wrong season," said Susan Klein. "Little later, most folks stand a tourist against the wall over there and throw knives as close as they can to them. See the stains on the floor? Makes the tourist real nervous."

The winter had been hard. Snow and cold alternating. Starving deer and elk were dying in the fields. The ranchers put out hay for them, but all the willow shoots had been browsed down and the animals couldn't digest the grass. They were starving to death with full bellies.

"You talk to that Morgan Martin," said Du Pré, "at that party. But you never tell me what she said."

"Morgan Taliaferro Martin," said Corey Banning, "to the likes of you and me. Oh, the Queen Bee and I admired the orchids and she, in her royal way, inquired gently as to just what the fuck it was I wanted. So I said that I was investigating these murders and did she have any employees she thought poorly of. She said she didn't employ people she thought poorly of. We drank very good brandy. The center of that bitch is frozen stone. No damn wonder sonny boy was such a hero. After growing up around her, not much would scare anyone ever again."

Du Pré laughed.

"You don't like her," he said.

"Actually," said Corey Banning, "I like her a lot. Strong women are my favorite. I must, however, find these swine who slaughtered six people so efficiently, and though the county is fairly well peopled, my nasty little mind has been reduced to essential thoughts. Like who is there competent enough to pull something like this off and tough enough to keep it hid. So my mind wanders back, inevitably, to the Queen Bee and her lovely sons. I had hoped for just a couple of psycho rednecks who'd get drunk and brag. I love guys like that. I hunger for 'em. But there ain't any around smart enough, unfortunately."

"Maybe they were not even from here," said Du Pré.

"Hogwash does not comfort me," said Corey Banning. "What I would really like to do is talk with Benetsee. I have flat picked the real world I am sentenced to to bits. I need that old man, get him to tell me what he sees in his world. But he's gone."

"I'm kinda worried about him," said Susan Klein.

"Oh," said Corey Banning, "he's just fine, I am sure. It's just he wants me to toss and turn at night and fret over him. He's doing this just to piss me off. I just know it."

Du Pré laughed. Whenever he had tried to pin Benetsee down, he felt like he was trying to nail water to the wall.

"Maybe he's there, home," said Du Pré. "Just decided to not leave no tracks in the snow."

Corey looked hard at Du Pré.

"I'm gonna go on out there," she said. "I'd appreciate it if you stayed here. No offense. Actually, I don't give a shit if it does offend you."

"You see him," said Du Pré, "you tell him Madelaine wants him to come and eat, do that often, he don't want to worry Madelaine."

Corey shrugged into her leather coat and pulled on her gloves. She nodded to Du Pré and Susan Klein and she left.

"How's Bart doin'?" said Susan.

"Ah," said Du Pré, "he is doing very well. He should have been a cop or a priest, you know, there is nothing that he likes more than to help people."

"Throw folks in jail when they fuck up so he can talk to 'em," said Susan Klein. "I think I get it."

"We don't have so very much crime here," said Du Pré. "Maybe some kids, they steal something. But then we got this, these murders, and this is some different."

"It is that. Listen, would you mind waving a shovel out round the door? Damn snow slamming down, I dunno anyone can find it now."

Du Pré got up and he walked to the door and took the

grain shovel leaning against the wall and he went on out. Snow splattered against the plastic and the translucent sheets bellied in the wind.

Du Pré shoveled the deep drift that had built up in the last hour away from the beaten path through the plastic sheets. The snow wasn't letting up and the tracks of Corey's big pickup were already half filled.

Du Pré saw some headlights glow in the white whirl and then the front end of Bart's Rover, thickly covered, nosed slowly up to him. Du Pré walked to the driver's window.

"And a fine spring afternoon to you," said Bart, as he rolled the window down. "Agent Ms. Banning passed me up the road a ways. I was doing about ten, she was doing about seventy. Split the difference, I guess she wasn't speeding. What's happening in the social center?"

"Just me and Susan Klein," said Du Pré. "We are just all waiting around for things to melt."

"All but the cattle," said Bart. "The calves are starting to come on. They like this weather, so they can be born and die the same day."

Du Pré nodded. He remembered all the calves he'd pulled and he could think of very few that hadn't arrived in a blizzard.

"Come on in, I will buy you a soda, coffee, something," said Du Pré.

Bart pulled round and parked and he got out and came to Du Pré, still shoveling.

"Snow'll have it back there in ten minutes," said Bart, "but the thought was nice."

Du Pré sighed. He threw one last shovelful off and they trudged back through the visqueen flaps and on into the bar.

Susan Klein set them up and they sat there in silence, sipping and waiting for nothing much. A truck ground up outside. Doors slammed.

Benetsee and Corey Banning came in. The old man was sopping wet; his ragged clothes ran water. He was smiling.

"She came by so fast she made me jump into the ditch," said the old man. "She drive like that, she come up on the rear end of a snowplow and kill herself."

"Pour some wine down this old bastard," said Corey. "I want to loosen his tongue."

Benetsee drank three very big glasses of fizzy screwtop wine. He belched and grinned. Susan Klein set a cheeseburger and fries down in front of him. He wolfed the burger down and then picked at the potatoes. She filled his glass and he emptied it in a long swallow.

"What do you see?" said Corey.

"Two pretty ladies, two men, a lot of snow," said Benetsee. "You want me to tell you who killed the people up in the mountains, who killed the people down here, all six of them, well, I can tell you that they are well liked by the coyotes."

Du Pré looked off, only half listening.

"Why's that?" said Corey.

"Coyotes don't tell me why they like them, just that they do. And you need to go now. Stay here, you get killed."

"Me?" said Corey Banning.

"Yes," said Benetsee, "but I don't know no more than that. You make this too much your fight. Lose sight of things."

Corey shrugged.

Du Pré felt the hair on the back of his neck rise.

If Benetsee said she was dead if she stayed, she would be. If that's what the coyotes meant.

"Other people, another time," said Benetsee, "some stories, people don't go all the way to the end. You know, people die, they go away, the story leaves them."

"Madelaine, she want you to come to dinner," said Du Pré, before Corey could speak.

109

"Yah," said Benetsee, "I got to talk her, anyway, so I go now, you come along later." The old man rose and drifted out the door.

"What you going to do?" said Bart, looking hard at Corey.

"Stay," said Corey Banning, "until I got this wrapped and knocked. My job. Danger's part of it."

"That does it," said Bart. "I think I'll see if I can get you pulled out of here."

"Listen good, you guinea son of a bitch," said Corey. "You can try and you can even maybe get me pulled out of here. You got a long arm. And what I'll do then is resign and go right on as a PI, for one lousy dollar. If I got to pay myself the dollar. Kiss my ass, Fascelli. You piss me off."

She walked out.

"Shit," said Bart. "She would."

"Yeah," said Du Pré. "I sure wish this damn winter would quit."

♣ CHAPTER 21 ♣

Some damn winter, this," said Du Pré.

Bart and Booger Tom and Du Pré were standing in the mud of a snowplow turnout, looking down on the lands below the bench. The Chinook wind had come, warm and thick with rain. The snows were melting, the creeks roared, the river was jammed with ice and out of its banks, and all the flat fields were flooded with water and sheets of ice. The cattle were soaked, their hair plastered; the horses snorted nervously and kept to the highest ground they could find.

"If it freeze bad," said Du Pré, "we will have some bad trouble."

"Ain't seen this since '49," said Booger Tom.

"The Gold Rush?" said Bart, sweetly.

Booger Tom looked at Bart for a long moment.

"Of course," he said. "I don't come to Montana till *after* they invented grass."

Du Pré looked down at the county road. Bill Stemple's pickup was struggling up it toward them.

"Hey, Bart," said Du Pré, "something is . . . Stemple, he would not come up to us unless he had to. Too much work he has now."

Bart went to his truck and he switched on his radio, shaking his head. He spoke into it for a moment.

"Let's go down," he said when he came back. "There's bits of cloth and I don't know what all washing out of Cooper Creek. Pieces of those idiots got killed by the avalanche. Stemple tried to get hold of me but I'd turned off my radio. The dispatcher couldn't raise me."

They drove down toward Bill Stemple, who turned off and waited.

Bart pulled up and rolled down his window.

"Howdy," said Stemple. "Listen, there's scraps of cloth floating out from under that mess of snow up the canyon there. I can't figure it. The cloth's been torn up, ripped. It don't look like the avalanche done it."

Bart nodded. "Puzzling," he said. He looked at Du Pré.

"How much cloth?" said Du Pré, shouting past Booger Tom, who was sitting in the middle of the seat.

"Damn near half a bushel," said Stemple, "strips and scraps."

"We'll be right along," said Bart.

They drove on down the hill. Stemple turned around and followed, not close. The road was either muddy or slick.

"What do you think?" said Bart, as they plowed on toward Stemple's.

Du Pré and Booger Tom shook their heads.

At the ranch they got on a pair of snow machines, Bart and Booger Tom, Du Pré and Bill Stemple, and slopped and roared up to the mouth of the canyon. Du Pré looked up at the deep, deep snow, melting down rapidly. The creek roared, high and brown.

He saw some bright red pieces of cloth float past. There were other pieces of ripstop nylon on the brown boiling water, stuck in the tangled branches of alder at the verge of the creek bottom.

Du Pré eased down the bank far enough to grab a couple scraps. He sidestepped back up the sodden bank and stood, turning the scraps around. He knitted his eyebrows.

"What?" said Bart.

Du Pré shook his head.

He walked over to Bill Stemple.

"You seen any them grizzly this winter?" he said.

"Oh, my God," said Stemple. "Not a sign. None."

"What the fuck are you talking about," said Bart, "that I can't know about?"

"Them male grizzly, they don't hibernate," said Du Pré. "I think that maybe one he was just napping when the avalanche it come down. So then he maybe get out of his den and he come on one of the people got killed. Eat them, then he just go on, under that snow. They were maybe all pretty close together. This cloth got some punctures in it, I think the holes made by bear teeth, myself."

"Hee, hee," said Booger Tom. "All winter long that damn bear there he has sack lunches under the snow. Didn't have to come out to the meat dumps."

"Oh, God," said Bill Stemple, "I shoulda thought of it. All those dead sheep we put there and a couple cows went tits up. I should have known."

"What meat dump?" said Bart. "I ain't following."

"We put them dead animal out so coyotes and bears eat them, don't bother the good stock," said Du Pré. "Worked good. Them Fish and Game people say it is illegal."

"I gather that the corpses in there are reduced to bear shit," said Bart. "Oh, they are gonna love this at USA Today. I think we have a good deal of the obnoxious press to look forward to. I suggest that we don't bring it up right away."

"No," said Du Pré, "I think you call a press conference maybe an hour from now, you do it by phone."

"Why?"

"It make such a big stink that the Governor, he will have to send people, dig around in there, otherwise we have to."

"I take your point," said Bart. "Although maybe all we have to do is put a screen across the creek here."

Benetsee say this country, this land hate these people, Du Pré thought. All my time here, I never know of anything like this now. But it did not kill me. It did not. It could have, but it held me for some time and it let me go. Up toward the light.

"Thanks," said Bart to Bill Stemple. They got on the snow machines, rode back down to the ranch.

Bart drove as quickly as he dared back down to the Sheriff's office. Du Pré went in and listened while Bart informed a news bureau of the day's startling events.

Then they drove back to the Toussaint Bar.

Benny and Susan were behind the bar, pulling beers and mixing drinks. The place was packed. The winter had been so miserable that no one had gone outdoors much, but the warm weather had come and spring and its mud and sleet weren't far away.

"It seems that a bear has been eating the unfortunates at the bottom of Cooper Canyon," said Bart.

113

"I know you don't drink anymore," said Susan, "so did you fall on your head?"

"Du Pré thinks the avalanche that buried the people also buried a grizzly sleeping in a cave or something. Then the bear crawled out and began munching. It's preposterous. I think he's probably right."

Benny looked at Du Pré for a long moment.

"Cooper Canyon is part of that big boar's country," he said. "I've seen the son of a bitch a couple times. He'll go twelve hundred, maybe."

"Can he just move through the snow?" said Bart.

"Easy," said Du Pré. "They are very strong. Pick up a bull and carry it, you know."

"Jesus," said Bart.

Du Pré nodded.

This is some place now, strange time, he thought, I am perhaps not seeing something. The ranchers they have killed, the country it has killed, but who was it shot the four people up in the mountains? Shot the wolves? Me, that I don't understand.

That time they thought about it, thought about it long time. They know this country, know it as good as me, lots of people know it as good as me.

Up there, big bear with a full belly sleeps under the ice.

Just shove his way through the snow, I have seen them in their strength.

Du Pré looked down suddenly at the drink Benny had set before him.

He lifted it and he sipped.

Some of my friends I fiddle for are murderers.

Them Fish and Wildlife people they kill that bear now, they will have to, the Governor, he will make them. Bad for the tourists, not so many will come.

My state is some kind of whorehouse now, I guess. I work in it. Take nice hot towels around.

I got to go and see Benetsee.

Du Pré rolled a cigarette and he lit it and he drew deeply. He drank.

What they do now? Try to dig what is left, those people, out?

I got to see Benetsee.

"Du Pré!"

Du Pré turned. Corey Banning was standing there, snifter of brandy in her hand. Her leather jacket was open. Du Pré could see her stainless-steel nine-millimeter in its holster on her belt.

"Are you all right?" she said.

Du Pré's fingers hurt.

He looked down. The cigarette had burned down between them. He dropped it on the floor, stepped on it, reached down, and picked up the butt.

"Thinking," he said. "It is very hard for me, you know."

"Strange business," said Corey, "the bit about the bear. You sure?"

"Pretty strange," said Du Pré, "but I don't know how else that cloth get all torn up. Them avalanche break bones but they don't do that, the rocks were covered in ice, no trees to tear them up, just brush in the bottoms."

She nodded.

"Corey," said Du Pré, "I think maybe everything has some changed, you know, I never had a time like this. Someday soon maybe the winds all smell different and I look at the stars on a clear night and the Big Dipper it is gone and there is something there I don't know."

"Well," said Corey, "things should start unraveling soon."

"Huh," said Du Pré. "Like them cloth, Corey? Only it don't unravel. It was ripped right apart."

She sipped her brandy.

They both looked at the floor.

❧ CHAPTER 22 ❧

The backhoe dug at the ice jam in the creek. The brown water started flooding through. There was a heavy fine-meshed net across the creek below. It was hung from two other backhoes' buckets, one on each side of the creek. When the chunks of ice were near, the operators lifted the net, let the ice pass, and set it down again. Strips of cloth were stuck in the net.

It was early April. The snow was melting back up the canyon. Earthmoving equipment had been brought in and National Guardsmen to operate it. The big machines were painted in desert camouflage.

A front-end loader dug at the collapsed snow and lifted its bucket. The big machine backed away.

"There," said Bart. He pointed.

The tail of a snowshoe stuck up from the bucket.

The operator backed away from the snowbank and he set the bucket down.

Bart and Du Pré walked over to the big machine. They looked at the snowshoe. It was twisted and the wooden frame was broken. Du Pré looked at the tail. It had been bitten. There were teeth marks, big ones, cutting right through the hard ash.

"There," said Du Pré.

Bart shook his head. He signaled the operator, who lifted

116

the bucket and dumped the load in front of them. The snow broke open. There was a pack still tied into the thongs, but the felt liner was gone and whatever foot might have been in it.

"Jesus," said Bart.

Du Pré shook his head.

Not much to say. So far we got not one scrap of a person but I don't know what we find, them grizzly got big strong jaws. Eat someone's head like it is an apple.

"You become Sheriff things get so interesting," said Du Pré. "I think I quit, change my name, move to Canada."

"Too late," said Bart, "or I'd join you."

Bart jammed the sharp end of a crowbar at the snow. It began to crumble. A glove appeared. Bart picked it up. He rolled the wristlet down. Some bones stuck out.

"Bingo," said Bart. "Now we call the medical examiner."

He trudged off toward a tent where there was a radio telephone.

Du Pré worked the frozen hand out of the glove. A woman's hand, a wedding ring and diamond on her left hand, there in the snow.

Du Pré reached in his pocket and pulled out a clear plastic bag and he sealed the hand and glove in it. He looked up at the loader. The operator backed away from the face of the slide. A long red stocking cap stretched between the bucket and the snow face. The hat parted.

Du Pré slipped and slid over to the snow face. He pulled out his sheath knife and chipped away around the edges of the hat.

He pulled the hat away.

Just white packed snow is all, he thought. I wonder, that damn bear he eat everything else?

Bart waved at Du Pré from the trail. Du Pré slid back down to him, holding part of the hat.

"They said for us to leave it alone," said Bart. "Better minds and much better men than the likes of us will take it from here."

Du Pré shrugged.

He handed Bart the plastic bag with the hand and glove in it.

"Just a minute," said Bart, walking toward the tent.

He came back empty-handed.

They walked down the muddy, icy track, stepping over big lumps of snow and gravel, to Bart's truck.

The mudlug tires threw slop and gravel hard against the truck's bottom shields. They wallowed down to firmer ground and out to the dry county road, and Bart got out and so did Du Pré to unlock the front hubs.

"Where you put that hand?" said Du Pré.

"On top of the sandwiches in the cooler," said Bart.

Du Pré nodded.

"It's a clear day," said Bart. "I think I'd like to fly up and look at the mountains."

Du Pré nodded.

"I'll go, too," said Du Pré.

I want to see who might be up them mountain. No one is trapping now, no one did too much this year, too bad. But there is someone who was up there when they set down them people and them wolf. That guy is crazy. The rest of it I don't know we ever know but I find out, that one.

Got to go up, got to come down, someone got to have seen something.

They went to the Toussaint Bar for lunch and had just finished their cheeseburgers when the Martin ranch's helicopter racketed in and set down on the bare brown softball field across the road. The picnic tables were still piled the way they had been in the winter, when the fools came for the service for the martyrs for the environment.

Du Pré and Bart ducked under the rotor wash and got in and strapped down. Taylor Martin revved the engine and they lifted off. It was a small, light machine, made for crop dusting and herding cattle.

Bart sketched out where he wanted to go on the pilot's knee pad of paper. Martin nodded and headed off toward the Wolf Mountains, hard and bright with snow, black-green forest running down the flanks like thick spilled paint.

They flew over the nearest high basin, unbroken white save at the edges where the trees held shadows. One tree shook and dumped its load of snow and the white clod sank and a lynx appeared, clutching the very top and glaring up at the noisy machine.

The pilot flew over to the north side and along the flanks of the mountains about a third of the way down. Some ravens were feeding on something in a thicket. They flew a bit and settled back down.

The pilot turned and flew over to the south side. The deep cleft of Cooper Canyon and its barren sides and the massive slide in the bottom appeared.

They went over a spur of the mountain to the next drainage.

Du Pré spotted some tracks.

"Skis!"

Bart leaned over and looked and he banged on the pilot's shoulder and pointed. The helicopter sank quickly toward the double line of tracks across the white. They went into thick growth a mile or so down the mountain.

The pilot dipped down lower and he went back and forth. The spur of the mountain ended in rock.

The tracks did not come out of the lower side.

He flew up the spine of the spur slowly.

The rotors roiled the snow below; it rose like a ground blizzard.

Du Pré stared.

"Have him go back up, find where he came up now," Du Pré yelled in Bart's ear. "Why this guy, he don't go down where he come up?"

Pretty simple, that, when you run a trapline it is a long circle or a U or something, so you got the most traps.

They rose up the slope till the mountain began to rise nearly straight up, broken masses of rock hard under the sky.

He didn't come over that.

They went to the right.

Nothing.

They went to the left.

Du Pré stared again. There was a small basin just above the treeline and the snow on it looked strange.

The wind had pretty well cleared it.

The pilot flew slowly around the edge.

Du Pré spotted some ski tracks at a place where the low trees had come in close.

"Go back down!" he yelled at Bart.

Bart scribbled on the pilot's pad.

The machine dipped and headed down, blades biting the gelid air.

They sank from winter to spring.

The pilot set down on the softball field.

Du Pré and Bart ducked out and ran and the machine rose and went off.

"The son of a bitch is still up there," said Bart.

Du Pré nodded.

"He'll wait till dark to come down," said Bart, "but he's only got so many ways he can come."

"He has a bunch of them," said Du Pré. "He get down

120

low and hide his skis he can cut across long ways. Take time but I don't think he will care."

"We call all them ranchers, see if there is a truck or car parked someplace," said Du Pré. "But I don't think so."

Bart nodded.

"Why be up there?"

"It is not far from where the people and the wolves were killed," said Du Pré. "This guy, I think he just wanted to see it again, you know."

"Why?"

Du Pré rolled a cigarette.

"He's a very tough guy," said Du Pré. "Knows this country good, you bet."

He smoked.

"Bart," said Du Pré, "he is very proud of what he did. He just maybe wanted to see where he did it again."

"Jesus," said Bart.

They walked toward the bar.

♣ CHAPTER 23 ♣

Du Pré squinted through the cold rising light at the mountains. He was hidden on a long sloping ridge, one with a good view to both sides. Anyone coming down the mountain for four miles on either side of him would have to cross the open sometime.

He glanced quickly back and forth. The air was dead still. He waved his smoky breath away from his face.

This guy he is out here. No car waiting on him. Nobody knows of anyone who was up there and I wonder he maybe drop from the sky. Somebody drop him from the sky.

Lot of damn work and it needs someone else who has a helicopter. Now who has one and who used it yesterday morning? Guy took us has one and he didn't take us till the afternoon. That guy, Taylor Martin, he was a war hero, Vietnam, flew choppers. Been over east there, his family, long as us Du Prés been here. Big ranch there.

Du Pré stood up. He switched on his telephone and dialed.

"Yeah," Bart whispered.

"That guy we look for he is gone," said Du Pré. "I think that Taylor Martin drop him off, take us up, bring us back down, go back up and pick him up."

"You know him?" said Bart. "Why do you think that?"

"Got to be someone pretty close," said Du Pré. "Chopper can't fly that fast. It's his, he don't fly out of an airport, just out of his hangar. Sixty miles away, you know. Now, he got a brother and a couple brothers-in-law there. Some of them people shot, they are killed near that Martin ranch. That bunch of people, they are burned, you know. Hot fire, someone made a firebomb, that car. Magnesium."

"Is there a reason that we are sitting out here playing soldier?" said Bart. "I'm cold. I'm hungry. And you say he's gone."

"You maybe call Corey?" said Du Pré.

"You call her," said Bart. "She likes reaming me out so much and I have a terrible headache. She's at . . ."

Bart read off the number. Du Pré hung up and dialed.

"Agent Banning," said Corey.

"It is me," said Du Pré. "I think maybe it is those guys, that Martin ranch out east, you know. "This guy we are looking for he was dropped off by a helicopter, you know, picked up, I think, too."

"Yeah," said Corey, "I know it's them. Can't be anybody else, but we haven't got any proof."

"You talk to them?"

"Oh, yes," said Corey. "I just did my best and the bastards looked at me like I was touched and needed some home cooking. Very clannish, they are."

"How come you don't tell us this?" said Du Pré, suddenly angry.

"Well," said Corey, "I'm a manipulative female and I thought if I let you alone you'd sort of stir things up."

"You tell me, I would stir things up some time ago," said Du Pré. "Don't you do this again."

Silence.

"Damn you," said Du Pré. "Them Martins, you think they maybe shot some of those fool kids, too?"

"You're very quick, Du Pré," said Corey Banning. "Now, don't fuck up. There's too many people over there who know. It'll come apart. But you go stir the shit they'll back into a circle, horns out, and it'll be another six months before it loosens up. I got to get them before too much longer or I'll be sent more help, and you know what that means."

Du Pré shut the telephone off.

I do not like this, I had thought she was more honest than that. But maybe she is right. There is more good weather coming. More tourists and fools and the way that this goes now maybe more dead people. Me, I don't got no answers.

Hell. Shit. Damn.

Du Pré walked down to his Rover and started it and sat in it smoking until the engine warmed.

I am a brand inspector, little rancher, grandfather, and a bit part, some cheap television movie.

But I did not make it like that, it was those foolish little bastards from the flat with all their silly notions, feel like they are better for this place than we are.

123

Du Pré reached under the seat and pulled out a fifth of whiskey and he had a slug and sat there watching the mountains and the sun spilling down them.

Can't find Benetsee, he is not around or not around when I come to find him, old fart. Leave him meat, tobacco, wine, he still won't come.

Here I am, cold morning, looking for a guy up there who was looking for something that he left behind that frightens him now. Or maybe just wanted to see . . . oh, I am a very stupid man. Not proud, scared, and two of them to do it.

Du Pré saw a car coming up the sloppy road behind him, a rental car pasted half over with mud.

Journalists.

Du Pré had another slug of whiskey. He rolled a cigarette.

Good headline. "Officers drink and smoke while so many lie dead."

They bother me, I will piss on their shoes.

Du Pré punched some numbers into his portable telephone and he waited a moment.

"Special Agent Banning," said Corey.

"More you are awake, longer your name gets," said Du Pré. "Now I am some mad with you. You don't lie exactly, you just don't maybe tell me all the truth you know. Well, I know something now which I am not going to tell you yet. Lead me someplace. I arrest somebody, I don't let you know and see how you like it."

"I'm trying to save some lives," said Corey.

"You still aren't telling me, you know, what," said Du Pré.

"Shit," said Corey.

"There are, you know, couple newspeople driving up toward me now, so I think maybe I tell them I spend time out here, freezing my ass, while them FBI don't tell me what they know, things are now interesting."

"You bastard."

"Oh, no," said Du Pré. "My parents, they are married three, four days before I come, my mother she hold her missal out on her belly, I pound on her stomach while she said she marry Catfoot. Me, I get there just in time always."

"Shit."

"Now, now," said Du Pré, "you maybe got this nice big thick file, the Martins, you let me see it."

"Goddamn you," said Corey Banning.

"Maybe we, how you say, do lunch," said Du Pré. "Now I got to go a minute here, soon as these newspeople get stuck."

Du Pré got out and looked down the muddy road and waited till the rental car got to a steep rise. It slowed and stopped while a spray of mud flared out behind. The rear end slid slowly to the edge of the road and off; the wheels settled and dug in.

Two people got out and looked helplessly at the car. They were dressed in funny clothes with pockets all over the arms.

Du Pré had another slug of whiskey and he rolled another cigarette and he got in his Rover and turned around and drove down the hill. The two reporters stood beside the car.

He drove past them, waving.

One of them screamed something.

Du Pré stopped the Rover, got out, walked to the back where they could see him, gave them the finger, and drove on.

This whole thing is now to come together, all them strings in knots and the ends followed into the shadows.

He glanced in the rearview mirror and the mountains

125

flamed in the sun, up high where the snow lay deep and would till July. The orange and red-pink of an abalone shell.

Du Pré stopped at the edge of the bench, where there was a turnout for the snowplows. He looked down at Stemple's ranch, the cattle in the pastures, Bill Stemple driving a tractor, unspooling a big roll of hay for his stock.

He could see all the way south to where the Missouri ran between its bluffs and gravel hills.

He looked off toward a shelf of rock in the high grass and sage. There was a pile of rocks on it, the slabs of limestone spalled off the mountains over time and time again. Piled about ten feet long and three feet high, littler slabs on top.

Plenty of holes to look through.

Two scouts could hide there and watch and there would be nothing visible if you looked up from below.

Du Pré got out and he walked to the fence and stepped through and he followed a game trail through the sage to the ledge and the pile some Indians had made so long ago.

The rock behind the pile was still wet.

Du Pré squatted down on his haunches.

He saw a cigarette filter tip.

Another.

A scrap of foil.

He got up and moved back and forth, looking at the ground.

Someone had crapped near a sagebrush.

Du Pré pulled a bag from his pocket and poked the turd into it with a stick.

He looked at a little left on the ground.

Raspberry seeds.

Somebody from right here, Du Pré thought. But me, I knew that.

✦ C H A P T E R 2 4 ✦

I was damn close," said Corey Banning, "and you got me and here it is."

She handed Du Pré a folder filled with sheets of computer type. Ugly stuff, Du Pré hated it. Always smelled like fluorescent lights, cheap floor polish, that paper.

"How much more they find up Cooper Canyon?" said Du Pré.

"Oh, scraps," said Corey. "That goddamn Governor swears to have the bear killed, right, and now the animal-rights idiots are picketing the statehouse. Anyway, folks want to die of pure dumbness and have a bear eat 'em, I don't care."

"Lot of medals, these two guys," said Du Pré. Taylor Martin and his brother Clark. Southdowns, probably, the Missouri people who came here to get away from the Civil War.

I meet these guys once, twice. Soft-voiced. Cattle, sheep, pretty big ranch. Both of them fly helicopters, both of them crash behind enemy lines, Vietnam, and both of them make it back. Volunteer a lot. Some trouble, get drunk in Saigon, beat the shit out of some MPs, lose rank, end up on the ground. Then they sign up, second tour for Clark, third for Taylor, they like it.

"Pretty good," said Du Pré. "Guys looking for the murderers are the murderers, they fly in and out. Nobody saw that some."

"I'm going out to reef on them," said Corey. "You want to come along?"

Du Pré nodded. He called Madelaine, told her where he was going.

Du Pré drove. He smoked. He reached under the seat and had some whiskey. He offered the bottle to Corey, but she shook her head.

"Not this time," she said.

"What you going to do you can't arrest them?" said Du Pré. "They don't talk to you, what?"

"Piss 'em off."

She will do that. Hope we all live through it, woman got a mouth on her like my great-uncle Hercule.

Du Pré shot down the lonely two-lane highway, swerving to miss the worst frost boils. A cock pheasant ran in front and into the sere weeds.

They drove for half an hour. Corey pointed to a pole covered in signs, each pointing to a ranch somewhere the hell and gone back in the rolling High Plains country.

Martin.

Du Pré turned and roared up a wide county road. A flock of ravens flew away from a dead deer by the side of the road. Antelope stood in the low swales in the folds of the hills, staring at the Rover as it shot past. Flights of ducks rose from marsh ponds that would be dry by July.

A fork in the road, another sign pole. Du Pré bore off to the right. Another ten miles and they found a mailbox atop a long welded chain, links the size of boot soles, "Martin" on the top. They turned off and drove up the rutted road and when they topped the second hill they saw the ranch, down in a stand of cottonwoods. Barns and sheds and three simple two-story ranch houses, railroad houses, bought as kits from Chicago factories, shipped by rail and then ox team to this place between the earth and sky, where there were no trees but cottonwoods, the lumber from them weak and useless.

Du Pré drove into the big yard. Tractors and machinery, seed bins, some chickens fluttering across the mud. A pair of blue heelers came out barking and circled behind the Rover, ready to bite the rear tires as soon as it stopped.

Du Pré sat for a moment. Corey opened her door and got out and she stood by the Rover, looking around.

A man came out of one of the machine sheds. He was wearing rubber irrigation boots and a red mackinaw and a yellow plaid hat. He walked slowly over toward Corey Banning.

"Special Agent Banning, FBI," said Corey. She held up her ID and the man came close and he looked for a long moment at the cards in the black leather case and he nodded and she put the wallet in her pocket.

Du Pré got out and he walked round to them.

"Du Pré," he said.

"The fiddler?" said the man. "You play right nice."

"I have some questions for you," said Corey. "Is there a place we can go sit?"

"How 'bout the truck here," said the man.

They got in.

Du Pré and the man sat in the front, Corey in back.

"I'm investigating the murders," said Corey, "of two Fish and Wildlife agents, two other men with them, on or about the evening of the sixteenth of November, and of two other people shot in October. Now, what is your name again?"

"Taylor Martin, ma'am," said the man, "like I told you before."

"You have a helicopter."

"Three of 'em," said Martin. "We run twelve thousand head here."

129

Jesus, thought Du Pré, that is one big damn bunch of cattle.

"You flew Du Pré here and Sheriff Fascelli over the Wolf Mountains yesterday?"

Martin nodded.

He wear that helmet and mask I don't know him, thought Du Pré. His hands are pretty steady there, though.

"Mind if I have a cigarette?" said Martin.

"Fine," said Corey.

Du Pré rolled one and lit it; so did Taylor Martin.

"It seems that someone was up in the Wolf Mountains, and that they could only have got in and out flying in a helicopter. You were with Du Pré and Fascelli part of that day. Where were you before and after?"

Taylor Martin blew out a long stream of blue smoke.

"Agent Banning," said Martin softly, "I shot two people who were cutting my fences and shooting my stock on the night of the twelfth of October, and then I burned them with a thermite unit I made."

"FUCKING FREEZE!" yelled Corey. She had her nine-millimeter jammed against Martin's head. "CUFF HIM!"

Du Pré took out his handcuffs and snapped them on Martin's wrists. Martin had turned slowly, so Du Pré could clip them behind his back.

"And then," he went on, "I flew up into the Wolf Mountains and I shot four men and six wolves. I chopped the slugs out of the bodies. Heads, actually, all of them, and then I flew back here."

"Christ," said Corey Banning. She was digging for her tape recorder.

"And I'll be perfectly happy to tell you everything you wish to know," said Martin.

"Call Bart and have him get a cell ready," said Corey. "I'll have to get transport for this guy, out to Billings."

"Let me out of this whatever-it-is for a minute," said

Taylor Martin. "My kid brother is in the shed there and he's got a rifle on you and I'd just as soon this all ended now."

Du Pré nodded and he got out and walked around the front of the Rover and he opened the door and helped Taylor Martin out.

"Clark!" yelled Martin. "I told them. I'm going now, it's over, go and finish feeding the calves in the third lot. I'll call you when I can."

Clark Martin came out of the building. He was carrying an assault rifle in one hand.

"OK, Taylor," he said. "Good luck."

The Martin brothers laughed.

Du Pré drove back down to the county road and then he cranked up to speed and when he hit the highway he drove at ninety, light bar flashing.

When they got to the jail in Cooper Bart and Benny were there, and they hustled Martin back to a cell after taking his clothes and giving him an orange jumpsuit.

Taylor Martin rubbed his wrists and he looked amused.

Corey Banning pulled a chair up to his cell and began to fire questions at him.

Martin answered all of them which did not mention anyone else. He maintained that it was only he who had shot six people.

"That's a lot of goddamned people," said Corey.

"I killed over three hundred in Vietnam," said Martin. "I have a true talent."

"Your brother helped you."

"Nope," said Martin.

"I'm going to keep asking questions till I know everything," said Corey.

Martin shrugged. "Could I have a soda? Flavor don't matter, a smoke, too."

Du Pré walked down to the fridge and got him one.

131

He lit a cigarette and passed it through the bars. Taylor Martin took the smoke and nodded at Du Pré.

Martin had a slug of pop.

"Bring me a pad of paper and a pen," he said. "I'll just write down what I have to say now and sign it. Or go away."

Du Pré fetched him a pad and pen and a clipboard.

Martin began to write.

"Agent Banning," said Martin, "I will write this, and it's pretty simple, really. And while I do I'm going to say a few things to Mr. Du Pré. He will, I think, understand them rather better than you."

"You don't talk like a ranch guy," said Corey Banning.

Martin laughed. "We have a uniform speech? My, my. No, we do not. I went to Yale, ma'am. Classics. With honors. So did my youngest brother. Clark went to West Point. So did one of our brothers-in-law. Other one went to Princeton, but every family has 'em, yes?"

"Vietnam?"

"I wanted to see what being a warrior meant," said Taylor Martin. "I did and I liked it."

"Do you like killing?"

Martin shrugged.

"I'm indifferent," he said. "It's either necessary or not, you know."

"You're lying about your brother."

"Nope."

He scratched on the pad.

"Mr. Du Pré," said Martin, "your people have been round here since when? 1870? 1886?"

"Eighty-six," said Du Pré.

"The second rebellion," said Martin. "We have been where the ranch is since 1879. Now it seems that our leases for summer grazing are to be terminated, on the whim of people who have never been here at all. A purely political decision, of course. It's the property of the United States government and therefore the people of our country, of course. But it was handled very badly and when those idiots came to cut fences and shoot cattle I thought I'd make an example of them."

Scratch scratch.

"Here," said Martin, handing the confession through the bars. "You need to sign as witnesses where I marked the two X's."

"Christ," said Corey Banning. "I don't believe any of this."

"Oh, but you must," said Taylor Martin. He took a drink from his can of pop.

"Bullshit," said Corey.

"The soda washed down a cyanide capsule," said Taylor Martin. "I suppose that you'll get in trouble for not checking the inside of my mouth. Too late now."

Corey Banning looked at him, stunned.

Taylor Martin smiled and then put his hand to his eyes and fell to the cell floor and died in a matter of seconds.

Du Pré pounded on his chest for a while, but it didn't do any good.

❖ CHAPTER 25 ❖

I didn't know he was so short," said Madelaine. She was looking at the Governor, who was squelching through the mud toward a portable podium. TV crews and reporters stood in deep ranks, waiting.

"Well, I have heard steers fart," said Du Pré, "and I do

not need to listen to this one sing, too. I think I will go to the bar now and have a nice drink. See there is a pretty woman there, buy her some pink wine."

"Poor guy," said Madelaine. "He can't be very happy, want a job like that."

They got into Du Pré's Rover and drove off to Toussaint in the gray spring rain.

"That Taylor Martin, why he do a thing like that?" said Madelaine.

"He was sick," said Du Pré, "some kind of cancer, maybe from that Agent Orange, they used it in Vietnam. Anyway, he confesses and then he kills himself. Now we got a confession and a dead end. Pretty smart guy, pretty tough, too."

"I wish all these people would go away," said Madelaine. "So angry, everyone, I never seen our friends and neighbors so mad."

Du Pré nodded. He shifted in the seat, scratched his neck.

"Only reason it is not much, much worse is that Bart and that Lawyer Foote they are very, very powerful people, they have kept too many of them FBI out of here. About twenty of those fools kicking in doors we have a real war. And now the Fish and Wildlife, they will let more wolves loose up there, and more wolves will get shot, and I suppose more people, too, you know. None of this, it would have happened, those people cared enough about what was here, find out a little what it is before they come."

"You are plenty mad, too, Du Pré," said Madelaine.

"Yah, well, I got to go fish dead people out of places here and there get buried alive, avalanche, I am a deputy which I swore I would never do, poor Bart is the Sheriff, we got to have a Sheriff, a rich man, otherwise we just get smashed. Lucky for us, he is here, a good guy."

"You didn't have time, make meat this fall," said Madelaine. "First time I know that happen."

Jesus, Du Pré thought, I shoot my elk, my deer, every year I am here since I was fourteen and I shoot deer before that. I shoot deer sometimes in the summer when Benetsee wants summer hides for his women relatives up in Canada, against the law but we got more deer here than we got jackrabbits. Deer carcasses, they keep the coyotes off the lambs. I don't make meat this fall, I ride herd on a bunch of mostly dead assholes should have stayed to home.

I hate these people, but kill them, no, that is wrong.

"It is a shitty mess," said Du Pré. "I would quit, you know, but I cannot do that, Bart."

"You cannot do that, you," said Madelaine. "This is plenty bad now, you know, but it will be worse, you quit. Bart quit, you quit, Governor send in his people, lot of shooting. Our friends, neighbors, very good shots. Also, they only want to live, so much."

"Huh?"

"You know what I am saying, Du Pré," said Madelaine.

Yah, I know, I am like that, too. I get mad enough, me, I don't care what anybody think. Kill Lucky, for sure. I almost kill that damn Bucky Dassault, too.

"Hah," said Madelaine. "Now that damn Governor, he worried about the tourists, you know, they will be afraid, not come to Montana at all. Maybe they get caught in avalanche, July, big old grizzly eat them under the snow. All those fat guys, Chamber of Commerces, having fits. Hah."

Du Pré laughed.

"Hey," he said, "we make maybe commercial, television. You want to die, come to Montana. We shoot you, feed you to the bears. Everything that walks, it is here, it bites."

"Don't get too mad, Du Pré," said Madelaine. "I know you pret' good, you don't get too mad, you get too mad, you talk, your Madelaine, before you do something."

"Ah," said Du Pré. He parked in front of the Toussaint Bar.

"I don't want to come visit you, Deer Lodge, or the cemetery, have to put flowers on your stone, say, Du Pré, you bastard, you were going to call your Madelaine."

She began to cry.

Du Pré put his arms around her and he held her and stroked her hair. She smelled of roses and mountain gentian.

"OK," said Du Pré, "I will do that. But you know, if someone is going to be having some shots at me I will have to talk to you maybe after."

"Well," said Madelaine, "that is all right, they shoot at you you just kill them, you hear, so you can talk, me, later."

Du Pré rocked her.

She snuffled and then fished around in her purse and took out a linen handkerchief and blew her nose and dabbed at her eyes. She never wore makeup.

"Pink wine," said Madelaine, "and I feel pretty lucky, so I roll for it with Susan."

They went in. The bar was empty but for Susan Klein and old Benetsee slumped down on a stool.

Du Pré yelled.

"Old man, I look for you, weeks, you old bastard, now you are here! I think you are white bones and coyote shit. Damn you!"

Madelaine ran to the old man and hugged him.

Benetsee turned round and he grinned his old brown grin at Du Pré.

"I been, Canada," he said. "I left you note, you know, hanging on a bush, behind my house."

Shit, Du Pré thought, I never went behind his damn house. The snow was deep. I never went far enough. Never went far enough. I am afraid of the snow now a little bit. A lot. Did not want my legs all the way down in it. Deep under that snow it scared me. Made me mad enough to live but it scared me. Damn, I ought to go burrow into it, sleep in it a few nights. Damn.

Benetsee's notes, they are carved in wood, bone, stone. His notes, very hard to understand. Easy to read, very hard to understand.

The old man lifted up a big glass of fizzy screwtop wine and drank it.

"Them people pretty good meat, Old Black Claws," said Benetsee. "I see him wake up under the snow, he grumble, claw his way out, find someone. Can't believe his luck, Old Black Claws. He eat pretty good there, couple three months. Hee. Sleep some, get up, go eat. Good life."

"God," said Susan Klein.

"Yeah," said Du Pré. "They hunt him down now for sure. Old bastard. I will miss him."

"He is gone," said Benetsee.

"Gone?" said Du Pré.

Gone fucking where? Them Wolf Mountain, they are an island range, it is hundred and fifty miles to next bear country.

"Where gone?" said Du Pré.

Benetsee belched.

"North."

Susan Klein set down Madelaine's wine and Du Pré's whiskey.

"Where north?"

"He don't tell me," said Benetsee.

"Old man," said Du Pré, "your help, I need now. What you know about these people killed? Who killed them? It is not right, you know. And we can't have more, you know."

"No more," said Benetsee, "of them. They all live now. Somebody else die but I can't see who."

Old man always knows the riddles.

I don't need this. Who dies? Bart? Me? Who?

"Yah," said Benetsee, "Old Black Claws, he eats them but he don't like them much, I guess. Except for candy bars in their pockets. Hee. Pretty damn bad when a grizzly don't like eating you."

"Oh, you awful old man," said Madelaine, "those people they got mothers, fathers, you know. Lots of tears, pretty awful, can't even bury their kids. Pretty awful."

"Them whites, they like to pickle their dead people," said Benetsee. "Pretty selfish. Lots of hungry Peoples out there. They take, they don't give back."

"Oh, barf," said Susan Klein. "Way you talk I ought to go dig up someone, fry them up, serve 'em to you."

She filled Benetsee's wine glass. He drank it.

"You have a cheeseburger now," said Susan, "or no more wine."

"Is this going to stop?" said Madelaine. "This horribles?"

Benetsee nodded.

"Sure," he said. "Everything stops, you know."

Du Pré looked down at the whiskey and ice in his glass. He could see a carving in the top of the bar, someone's initials, very old and filled with black polished dirt. The bar top was more than a century old.

"Hey, Susan," said Du Pré, "looking down through his glass, "how old, this old bar here?"

"Made in Pennsylvania in 1868," said Susan, "this and the backbar. Old German woodcarvers. Shipped to Fort Benton and when that died out it was hauled to Miles City and then here. Got dates on the back of the far left door there, where the old ice blocks were kept. All zinc in it, like the ceiling here."

HDP, the carving said. My ancestor, Hercule Du Pré, the one who did cuss so very good, him, he sat here, carve his initials in this wood.

138

He say goddamn, shit, Balls of Christ, all that.
Me, I say it, too.

✤ CHAPTER 26 ✤

Du Pré and Bart looked up the Cooper Creek Canyon. All mud and rock now, a couple bloated carcasses of mountain goats that had died when the avalanche came down.

One of the medical examiners stood next to them, puffing on a pipe. He was young, moustached, very calm.

"The bear didn't eat the lower jaws," the ME said. "Nice of him. We were able to identify all of the victims. If he had we would have been mixing and matching teeth till the next millenium."

Du Pré nodded.

Good for that Old Black Claws. Hope he walks all the way up to Canada and finds himself a nice ski hill to feed off of. Nice fat young yuppies. I send him a case of hot sauce or something. This is pretty terrible but pretty funny.

"Yeah, well," said Du Pré, "that Governor he send in his trappers and hunters and they don't find Old Black Claws, but I guess they shoot some other bear and call it even."

"Governors are like that," said the ME. "Offering a million-dollar reward for information leading to the conviction of the murderers of the people killed here last October is another example. Would you care to bet that someone is convicted?"

"No," said Du Pré.

"You're all done with this now?" said Bart. The torn

ground was trampled by searchers. The ice had scraped off the brush, tearing the roots out when the moving equipment had lifted it.

"Eight death certificates," said the ME. "I suppose I'll be back here soon. For one thing, it strains credulity to think that Taylor Martin murdered six people without assistance."

"I just want to know who killed the two in my county," said Bart. "I have very modest ambitions."

"Well," said the ME, "one of them died instantly. A Magnum rifle shot through the brain, but it hit the stem. Magnum rifles are useless, of course, for shooting much of anything; they just punch a hole through. But the woman didn't die right then. Someone cut her throat. She was alive till her jugular was separated."

"There was not that much blood, that car," said Du Pré.

"There's been plenty of time to wash up," said the ME. "There are some chemicals that reveal minute quantities of blood. But without a tip you won't know where to look, and if you do get a warrant and you can find some blood there still probably won't be enough to type even if there is enough to declare it human, which I doubt."

"I wonder if we will ever know," Bart said.

"Murderers are an unremarkable lot," said the ME. "They kill when they are angry, or for money, or in a botched robbery, or jealousy. If you haven't found out anything by now I don't think you will find enough to get any convictions, since your confession will come from someone who was a part of it. You have to have corroboration. There won't be any. And there isn't any *reason* for anyone to come forward. Nobody's talked by now, I don't think anyone will."

"Very encouraging," said Bart.

"Taylor Martin's confession foxed you," said the ME. "Now you have to go *around* that. Even the vaunted FBI is at a loss. That formidable Banning woman, by the way, is dangerous.''

"Eh,'' said Bart.

"I don't happen to be from Montana,'' said the ME, "and I love it here. I love the people, too. I even love the fact that they are crazy. My brother was an officer in Vietnam, and when he arrived, a fresh second lieutenant, out in the boondocks, the staff sergeant took him aside and saved his life.''

"Huh?'' said Bart.

"The sergeant said, son, these are Montana and Wyoming boys here. You ask them to do something, they'll probably do it. You order them, they'll kill you. Last officer ordered them lasted seven hours. My brother was polite to his men and he lived because of them. This Banning woman is from here, and she's getting pissed, and I fear she may saddle up and charge just to see what she can shake loose. Even unlawfully. I would recommend that you request her transfer.''

"She talk to you?'' said Bart.

"Frequently,'' said the ME. "She has four suspects. She's probably right, but the days when you could bung suspects into a cell, let them sit in the dark, and then use the rubber hoses are long gone. That is only done in graduate schools now. But she just may do something out of anger and it will not be the right thing.''

"She is one girl who hates to lose,'' said Du Pré.

"Get her out of here,'' said the ME.

He walked off, in his rubber boots.

"What do I do about this?'' said Bart.

"Huh, ah,'' said Du Pré, "well, we are some her friends, we maybe talk with her?''

"Worth a try. All we need now is an FBI agent getting blown away,'' said Bart. "I thought she was sent here to *avoid* that.''

141

Du Pré shrugged.

This Corey Banning has been looking very tired and she is not letting us know that she knows anything even if she don't know anything.

"Maybe we let that Madelaine of mine talk, her," said Du Pré.

"OK," said Bart.

They squelched back to their four-wheelers and backed and filled, tires sucking out of the mud, and went down the wrecked road toward Cooper.

Children were playing soccer on the softball field. The trees were in bud, cannily waiting out the several frosts between here and the summer. Du Pré saw a long flight of geese headed straight north, the lead goose homed on the polestar even in high sun.

Du Pré and Bart parked in front of the Sheriff's office and went in. Bart tried to raise Corey Banning on his phone, then called the FBI office in the trailer.

"I don't have anything to say to you, fuckhead," Bart said to whoever was on the other end of the line. "Just tell Banning we are at the Toussaint Bar and have some items of interest to discuss with her." He hung up. "I'm usually a nice man."

Du Pré nodded.

They drove down to Toussaint. Corey Banning's muddy rig was already parked out front.

"I go get Madelaine," said Du Pré to Bart, out the window of his Rover. He drove off to her place, his, too, now.

She was sitting at her beading table in the living room, picking through jars of beads, looking for the perfect shade to add to the hatband she was making for her son.

"I need you, my love," said Du Pré. "Come talk that Banning woman, she is I think about to maybe get herself in trouble."

"OK," said Madelaine, "but I don't know what I say."

"Oh," said Du Pré, "maybe just listen, you do that good for me."

"All people really need," said Madelaine. "They talk through it mostly."

Du Pré nodded.

She screwed the lid on a little jar of beads and she shrugged into her jacket and they went out and down to the bar.

Bart and Corey Banning were sitting off at a table. They weren't talking. Bart was looking a little off to the right, Corey a little off to the left. Bart got up and walked to the bar the minute Madelaine began to move toward them.

Madelaine stood for a moment. She said something in a low voice and she laughed and sat down. Corey bent to listen. Madelaine whispered. The two women got up and came round so that they could sit with their backs to the rest of the saloon. They put their heads together.

"Well," said Bart, "we're pretty worthless here. I need to run out to my place and see that old misery Booger Tom and sign some paychecks. Are you gonna go look at the spot where our two came to rest? I wonder if we missed anything last fall."

"OK," said Du Pré.

Yeah, we miss something last fall. You miss something, every time. But now maybe the water and spring it move it down to the little creek or stick it on the uphill side of a sagebrush and maybe now I see it. You can hope, anyway.

Du Pré waved to Madelaine and he went out and drove back up the bench to the turnoff above the draw where the four-wheeler and the two dead fools had been dumped fifty years ago, it seemed.

I like to see that snow go away, Du Pré thought, maybe I move, the damn desert.

Du Pré walked to the rock and then he let himself down hand by hand, grabbing on to sagebrush till he

143

was at the spot where the two dead kids had been. The marks in the earth had mostly erased. A few chips of glass on the ground. Du Pré squatted and looked hard, looked up at the sky. A raven flew past.

Been a badger through here, couple days gone.

Smell the new grass.

Something's not right here.

That root there is too straight.

So is the other one.

I wonder.

Du Pré shuffled over to the sagebrush.

He reached down and picked up a nail. One for a horseshoe. Never been used on a horse, though.

Another. Another. Another.

Du Pré stood up. He put the nails in his pocket and he went back up the hill to his Rover and drove off.

✤ CHAPTER 27 ✤

Du Pré," said Packy, "you're nuts. I couldn't make it down that hill with this leg. And you act like I'm the only man in the damn county has a use for shoein' nails. Is this all because of that dog? Jesus, man, I found the dog thirty miles away."

"I tell that Corey Banning she is all over you like stink on shit," said Du Pré, "so you better think good and you better have some other people they know where you were that damn night, you know."

"I pulled shoes till fucking two in the morning," said Packy. "I did it three different places. You know me, I just

make my rounds and send my bills out and that's it. I didn't
see anybody. They were out or they were asleep."

"Which places you do that at?" said Du Pré.

"Stemple's. They was off in Billings, you know. Then I
did some at Moore's, till about ten at night. Then I went
way the hell out to the St. Francis place. I hate those bastards and they take lousy care of their stock, but I got to do
what I can. I love horses."

"And they were in jail that night," said Du Pré.

"Well," said Packy, "they are a lot. But the lights were
on in the house and there was a pickup there I didn't know.
It was dark, I didn't look at the license plate. It took a long
time to catch all the damn horses and it was after two-thirty
when I finished."

Du Pré nodded.

"Packy," said Du Pré, "if you are lying even a little bit
you got to tell me now, for Chrissakes. This is a very bad
business. People around here they got to know some who
did this. OK? Them FBI they will not go away, me and Bart
we won't stop. We can't, they can't. It was wrong, that.
They cut fence and shoot stock we arrest them, make them
pay. But not that."

Packy raised his hands. They were covered in scars,
white memories of cuts and punctures from his hard work.
A couple fresh red holes.

"OK," said Du Pré, "I will do this. I will tell that Banning about the nails but not about you. She probably figure
that out, you know. I got to do that that way, you know."

Du Pré rolled a cigarette and lit it and he smoked a moment.

"OK," he said, "you are at the St. Francis place, you see
this pickup. Now, they got some other trucks out there.
Any of them gone, you know?"

Packy shook his head. "They had a couple old beaters,
didn't even license them, used 'em for hauling on the

ranch. Never took 'em off of it. Then they had that canner truck."

"Oh, Jesus Christ," said Du Pré, "I forgot about that."

The St. Francis brothers bought dead animals for the dog food canners and the rendering works. They had a truck with a stainless-steel bin on the back, one that could be steam-cleaned. Winch and tackle.

I bet that cable was long enough to let that damn car with them two dead people in it down into that gully. Careful, so it don't catch fire.

"The pickup," said Du Pré softly. "What can you remember? Light? Dark? You tell what make?"

"I don't know new trucks so good," said Packy. "It was dark and it had a low camper cap on it and that's all I remember. I was tired as hell and I hardly looked. I don't know whether the canner truck was there or not."

It damn sure wasn't there.

I find out who run that truck when the St. Francis brothers are in jail or busy sometime other way, you bet.

"OK," said Du Pré, "I think I tell that Banning now about your nails down there, in the gully."

"They weren't mine," said Packy. "Damn it, they weren't mine."

"We got to find out some things," said Du Pré. "You better come with me, I guess."

"Christ."

"It is better than she come for you, maybe with some them fools she got stuck down in the trailer," said Du Pré.

Packy got into Du Pré's Rover, and they drove down to the trailer park where the FBI was parked.

Corey Banning's big diesel pickup was parked out front.

Du Pré and Packy got out and walked on in. Corey and her three assistants looked up from their desks. Du Pré nodded.

146

"We got to talk, Corey," said Du Pré.

Corey got her coat and put it on and they went back out and sat in Du Pré's Rover. Every other second a face appeared at the trailer window.

"OK," said Du Pré, "I went back out, the place where those two people found dead, up on the bench there. I find some horseshoe nails, I go to talk to Packy, he says they are not his, he did not put them there."

Corey looked at Packy impassively.

"That night Packy say he is shoeing, I mean taking shoes off for the winter, he does horses at Stemple's, at them Moores', then goes on out to the St. Francis place. They are in jail we know. But Packy he see a pickup there, one he don't know. Don't know there, anyway. And then I ask him, other trucks the St. Francis got? He says, they got a canner truck."

"Holy Christ," said Corey Banning. "Who else drives that truck when the St. Francis brothers are in the jug?"

"Me, I don't know," said Du Pré. "I miss that, I don't sell my dead horses, I bury them, I sign off horse shipments but I don't sign off dog-food horses already dead. I live here all my life, I know them St. Francis do it, but not who does when they cannot."

Corey Banning nodded.

"Got a nice long winch on it," she said. "I don't think that they thought it would get seen. Didn't think we'd use choppers."

"No," said Du Pré, "it wasn't important. If the dead people, their truck are found, Martin wants it found."

"That's a conspiracy," said Corey Banning. "Bingo. They means conspiracy."

Du Pré nodded.

"Other thing, I think that these people knew that those little fools were coming, and they spotted them and they followed them. Killed them. Make a point, them."

"Uh, huh ho ho," said Corey Banning. "And who here lives in both worlds?"

"Yeah, I guess we know now," said Du Pré.

"Whaddya think, Packy?" said Corey Banning. She grinned at him.

Packy looked blank. He looked away.

"I'm scared," he said. "I'm accused of something horrible. And you think I did it."

"Nope," said Corey Banning, "I don't think you did anything bad, Packy. Not at all. Not a moment. What I think, you little fucker, is that you know something you ain't telling us. Not even something you saw. Something you heard, I think. What did you hear, Packy?"

"Hear?"

"You move around a lot, Packy," said Corey Banning, "and the weather wasn't all that bad, the fall here. Why the fuck are you out there till three in the morning?"

"I do that a lot. It was dry, I do that a lot."

Corey Banning nodded.

She looked off into the distance.

"Who drives the damn truck, Packy?"

"The canner truck?" said Packy. "I do."

"*You do*," said Du Pré. "You son of a bitch, you quit playing your fucking games with me. Damn you."

"Look," said Packy, "I didn't do it and I just don't know if that truck was there that night. That's all I said. Now I'm tired of being yelled at. Take me home, damn it."

Du Pré looked at Packy. He looked at Corey Banning.

"Let him go," said Corey. "But, Packy, you stick around. And if I ask you a question, you bastard, you give me an answer. All of it."

Packy got out of the Rover and he limped off.

Du Pré rolled a cigarette. He lit it, offered a pinch of tobacco out the window.

148

"Give me some, too," said Corey Banning.

She did the same, mumbling.

"These people who were killed," said Du Pré, "they belong to some group want to take the West, make it over for them. That group decide, this night, we cut fences, we shoot cows. Maybe all of them aren't killed, maybe some they chicken out, you know."

Corey Banning nodded.

"At last," she said. "Useful work for my three dear friends in the trailer. Who's a member of Earth First or whatever who is also from here?"

"I hate this," said Du Pré. "I could maybe take them being mad. Not waiting on these kids like that, I cannot take that."

Corey held out her hand for Du Pré's tobacco and they smoked for a while. Du Pré reached under the seat, had some whiskey, put it back.

"Packy," said Du Pré, "he is some scared, you know."

"He should be," said Corey Banning.

"I am scared, too," said Du Pré.

"You should be, too," said Corey Banning.

"Why, you think?" said Du Pré.

"'Fore this is over we are all going to find out things about our people we will really wish that we did not know," she said.

✤ CHAPTER 28 ✤

I don't give a shit you don't like it," said Bart.
Both of the St. Francis brothers were standing beside

their canner truck. It was a lot bigger than the two of them, so Bart and Du Pré could look at it anyway.

"How much cable you got on this thing?" said Bart.

"What's it to you?" said the St. Francis on the left.

"Listen, asshole," said Bart, "if I got to go get a warrant I'll be pissed off and I'll get a nice fat one and toss your fucking house, too. Now, how goddamn many feet of cable?"

He was looking at a big winch mounted on a high frame at the rear of the truck bed, over the stainless-steel bin.

"A hundred and fifty yards."

"Pull a couple ton?"

"Yeah. We never had to, but it could."

Bart walked over to the truck and he swung up to the winch drum and he grabbed the hook and undid the brake and pulled out three feet of it.

"My, my," said Bart. "Which one of your dead horses had dark green paint on it?"

"What?" said the same St. Francis.

"I said your fucking truck is impounded. Now get me the goddamn keys."

Du Pré raised his eyebrows.

So now we are going out the other side, the fog.

I liked it better in there, but the sun, it always come up, burn that fog away.

Now I carry that other nine-millimeter, too.

Shit.

"The damn keys are in it."

"I'll call you when you can have it back. There gas in this turkey?" said Bart. He looked blood mean.

"Full tank."

"You want to flip, see who drives the hearse?" said Bart.

"Nah," said Du Pré, "you can do it."

"What if I order you to?" said Bart.

150

"Ah," said Du Pré, "I guess you can still drive it, you know."

"I thought so," said Bart.

He clambered down and got in the cab and started the truck. It was well tuned and settled into a rolling hum quickly.

Du Pré drove on ahead to Cooper. He unlocked the gate at the impound lot and waited. It took Bart another fifteen minutes to get there.

"I believe we will share our newfound lead with our FBI friends," said Bart.

"Good," said Du Pré. "She scream when we don't do that."

They went in and called Corey Banning's office. She wasn't there. The flunky on duty patched Bart through.

"The meat wagon from those asshole St. Francis brothers has a cable winch. There is dark green paint on the three feet of cable just above the hook. The four-wheeler pulled out of the arroyo was dark green on the bottom. I think we have our first piece of actual evidence, if I can guess what evidence is."

"Sounds good," said Corey Banning. "Cut it off and send it to the State Crime Lab boys."

"It's late in the twentieth century," said Bart. "I believe there are girls there, too, actual medical examiners and like that."

"Anything else need to go?" she said, ignoring him.

"I'd say the whole thing. The bodies may have been hauled in the bin in back. It looked spotless. But you never know."

"Very thorough. Who's going to drive it over there?"

"How about one of your guys?"

"I wouldn't really trust them with a rubber duck," said Corey, "but if you insist."

"I do."

"OK."

"Where are you, anyway?" said Bart.

"Up on the bench."

"OK," said Bart, "why are you up on the bench?"

"Following Packy around. Just want to see if I can make him run a little."

Du Pré looked idly at the speakerphone on Bart's desk.

So many damn gadgets here now today. I don't like any of them.

"Well," said Bart, "you want to come in and look at this?"

"Nah," said Corey, "I'll call one of my bozos."

"OK," said Bart.

The speakerphone sounded with shattering glass and then popping sounds and then silence and gurgling.

Bart and Du Pré looked at each other.

"Oh, my God," said Bart.

They ran out to Du Pré's Rover. He gunned the engine and switched on the light bar and they shot along the road fast enough for the rear end to wallow.

"The damn bench is only twenty miles long, fer Chrissakes," yelled Bart. "*Where* on the bench? Where's the phone, damn it, I'll call Booger Tom."

Bart dialed and waited and waited and then he shouted into the phone.

"Not there," he said, shutting it off. "Booger Tom says Packy went on toward the Stemple place when he drove away, but he didn't talk to him so he isn't sure really where he was headed."

Du Pré turned to miss a dead porcupine and then swerved back. He gunned the engine again.

"I go down below and you watch the line up there," said Du Pré. "We can see a car easy, there is no trees there."

He took a fork in the road and raced back down to the county road in the bottom flats. Bart scanned the line of road up on the bench.

They drove and drove.

"There!" Bart said, pointing.

Corey Banning's big diesel pickup was up near a gravel pile on the bench road. Du Pré roared onto a cutoff that led up to it. They flew coming up over the top. Du Pré braked hard and they skidded to a stop behind her truck.

The rear window on the driver's side was shattered.

Du Pré went to the right, Bart to the left, guns out, looking at any nearby cover.

Du Pré looked in the cab.

Corey had fallen over toward the passenger seat, most of her head blown away. Her hair was thick with clotted blood. The phone was still in her hand.

"Damn," said Du Pré. "Now the shit really hit here."

He turned away and breathed heavily.

Pile of rocks down there in the field.

Rifle barrel sticking though them.

"Get down, Bart!" Du Pré screamed. He jerked one of his nine-millimeters from his holster and squeezed off several rounds at the rocks. Keep his fucking head down, you bet.

A slug slammed into the grille of the truck and whined off.

She probably had a rifle, that truck somewhere, Du Pré thought. He squirmed backward and reached up and opened the door.

A black hole appeared, just below the handle.

Very nice assault rifle, on clips in there, couple extra stacks for it.

Du Pré pulled it out.

He slithered over far to his right and edged slowly

through the rank green grass at the edge of the road.

He set the sights on the rocks and he waited.

The rifle barrel moved a little.

Right there.

I hit that it ricochet on through, if he is aiming it, it kill him maybe.

Du Pré waited.

"Du Pré!"

"Yah, Bart!"

"What do I do?"

"Stay back, don't get shot."

There. I see that damn barrel twitch a little. I know.

Wish my eyes was good like I was twenty.

The barrel moved a little.

Du Pré squeezed off six rounds.

The barrel was gone.

"OK," said Du Pré, "I am going down the hill now. You stay back, you know, I got a better gun."

Du Pré coiled around, stood up and ran downhill suddenly.

Nothing moved there.

He went down to his knees and slammed onto his belly and snaked through the sage and grass.

He edged slowly around the rocks.

A hand, outstretched.

Gun stuck up on a sagebrush.

Du Pré stood up and moved around slowly.

"Damn," he said, looking down. "I want to arrest you, Packy, and I say no to myself, and then you do this. Shit."

He looked back up the hill.

No Bart. He must be calling.

Oh, shit.

Bye, Packy.

✤ CHAPTER 29 ✤

Du Pré sat on Benetsee's porch, leaning against the woodpile. His boots were in the iris shoaled round the old man's shack. Plants here grew well and close. The old man never tended them.

Du Pré rolled a cigarette and snapped his old brass lighter till it caught. Some hairs from his moustaches turned to ash in the flames. He inhaled tobacco and rank stink. He blew the mingled smokes out.

Ah, old man, I need you, I do not know what to do. Corey Banning, FBI, gets her head blown off and I kill poor Packy and now we got a dead FBI and a dead end and we got maybe fifty FBIs headed here and not even Bart and Lawyer Foote can stop them when one of theirs been killed. Even if the killer is killed, too.

Me, I know out there all them soldiers come back from some wars, they are looking to their guns and making sure they got the ammunition, take a lot of FBIs with them, and out there in the sheds and attics of my friends and neighbors there are assault rifles and machine guns and heavier stuff, too.

The Constitution, it say the government may not stop the people from having arms. Then the government, it argue, well, no machine guns for you or heavy artillery, bombs, grenades, bazookas, even sawed-off shotguns. We government, we can have them, but not you.

My friends and neighbors some say bullshit, Christ, I got

no idea what they got out there, but I got, me, in my attic that MP-40 Catfoot bring back from the Second World War, I got that Russian assault rifle I buy and take to Dave the gunsmith who files down the sear and I got twenty-twenty five thousand rounds of ammunition for them both, nine-millimeter and the long cartridges in that funny curved clip, and I got fifty pounds of dynamite and diesel fuel and fertilizer and I can easy make a great big bang I want to.

There is somewhere around here two hundred them onetime rocket grenades, stolen from that Great Falls Armory. Couple twenty-millimeter cannon not counting the ones on that old warplane, that Lightning P-38, keeps driving the FAA nuts 'cause it is not registered but it is out there fully armed. I don't know who got that.

That's just the stuff I know about.

Corey Banning's brains splattered on the dashboard.

Packy not got no face when I get through with him, them rock chips see to that.

Time of the Blood Moon. Time of Sorrow.

They hurt my Madelaine, they hurt my Jacqueline, my people, I will kill every one of the sonsofbitches myself. Me, I am sick of these assholes, we were doing pret' good before some shitheads from the flat come here and cut fence, shoot cattle, get the government put them wolf up in the mountains. It is like you are leaned over your kitchen table some Sunday morning, bunch of preachers kick your door down, bang a gong make your headache worse, go through your whole house and when they are done then they stay, how nice, we will just live here, help you. You can be just like us.

Shit. Shit. Shit. Shit.

Goddamn twentieth century.

Nineteenth wasn't so fucking wonderful either.

Hope that Bart, he can keep his temper, too, he got one,

them FBIs come here now they are out for blood. Don't care whose long they get some and a promotion, bigger office.

It is all so wrong.

Never would have happened, them fools stay home, don't come here, do what they did.

Du Pré heard the bull-roarer. He went around back to the sweat lodge. The flaps were up. The sound of the cedar shake on its rawhide string bellowed and died and bellowed again.

Old Benetsee, out from the house a ways, behind the lilacs and the red willows.

Du Pré walked through the bushes. The old man was squatting in the shade. A younger man, short and stocky, was whirling the bull-roarer overhead and Benetsee was either nodding or raising a finger. When he raised the finger the younger man stood up on tiptoes and put all of his strength to the task.

Du Pré squatted down beside Benetsee and he waited. The old man would speak when he wished to and not before.

They watched the apprentice for a while. Finally Benetsee stood up. The young Indian slumped wearily and the bull-roarer flapped to silence.

"Go out to this man's car," said Benetsee. "There is some wine in it. Some tobacco. Food."

"Just wine," said Du Pré.

The young man stretched for a moment and then he walked away.

"Pret' bad things," said Benetsee.

Du Pré nodded.

"They get a lot worse," said Du Pré.

"Maybe not," said Benetsee. "Maybe I go and talk with them."

"Huh?" said Du Pré. "You remember last time? They

157

come here, I have to jam my gun, a neck, before they remember their fucking manners. Why you think they got better, last week?"

The apprentice came back with the wine and a big canning jar. He poured Benetsee a staggering draft and set the jug down and went off out of sight behind the trees over the little creek.

"You got a very bad temper, my son," said Benetsee.

Never call me that before, Du Pré thought. I be getting some good advice now, you bet. Probably better than I want to hear.

Pretty crazy, all around here now. Watch the earth go mad, maybe. I could use a big earthquake.

"Well," said Benetsee, "maybe we go on down to Susan's, get me a cheeseburger. You know, I have two young men show up this morning, long hair, expensive clothes, they want to go on vision quest."

Du Pré waited.

"I send them, Benjamin Medicine Eagle, he does that sort of thing."

Du Pré laughed.

"What they say?"

"Nothing," said Benetsee. "I tell them, me, I do only circumcisions. Benjamin Medicine Eagle, he is their man."

Du Pré howled. He roared.

"We go now," said Benetsee. He stood up, scratched the back of his neck.

Benetsee went into his shack and he came out with the red nylon envelope that held the eagle's wing he had taken from the fools in winter. He swung the flat red package by a loop at one end, idly.

"Ah, good," he said. "We smoke now."

Du Pré rolled and lit two cigarettes and then he drove off toward Toussaint.

There were four government car-pool cars parked out in

158

front of the bar, and eight men standing by the front door. Susan Klein was standing in the doorway, shaking her head.

Du Pré pinned the badge on his leather jacket. He and Benetsee got out. The FBI agents turned and looked curiously. One of them came round the hood of the far right car, walking easily, a tall, very dark man.

Lot of Indian blood, him, thought Du Pré. The man glanced off to his right.

Long earlobes. Lot of Indian blood.

"Special Agent in Charge Harvey Wallace," said the agent, extending a hand to Benetsee. "How are you, Uncle?" He looked down at the ground politely, waiting.

Couple minutes now, Du Pré thought, then Benetsee speak. This FBI is Indian some. Knows to respect the old, they know things.

"You long way from your people," said Benetsee. "You go back there often."

The agent nodded.

"I'm Wallace in white world," he said, dropping into Blackfeet. "I am Weasel Fat in Indian."

"Ah," said Benetsee. "We maybe go talk to Susan, there, she is some upset, I know, maybe smooth things down. Less noisy."

"Good," said Harvey Wallace.

The two men walked over to Susan Klein, still blocking her front door. Du Pré followed. The other agents looked at him, looked away after they spotted his Sheriff's badge.

"Afternoon, ma'am," said Harvey Wallace to Susan. He turned and passed Du Pré and began to speak very quietly to the men. They got in the cars and went off in opposite directions, two cars each one.

Harvey Wallace, Du Pré thought. This is one tough son of a bitch.

Du Pré was still standing outside. Harvey Wallace walked

up to him, rubbing a long finger on the side of his nose, looking at the ground.

He looked up suddenly. Very black eyes, very sad ones.

"Gabriel Du Pré," he said, "Corey Banning thought a lot of you. She respected the spot you were in, too. This is a very bad business. And I need your help."

Du Pré waited.

"We must uphold the law," said Harvey Wallace, "and I am charged with doing that and I will. And it must be done in such a way that we don't start a war."

Du Pré let out his breath.

"Do us all a favor," said Wallace, "and don't kill anybody else. Poor Packy might have led us to the killers. Might not. I know he was shooting at you, but in future, please just run. I need suspected killers and their accomplices alive. Dead, they merely pose more questions."

Du Pré nodded. Well, me, I don't back away, a fight, so good.

"Let me buy you lunch," said Harvey Wallace.

✣ CHAPTER 30 ✣

M aybe they've changed," said Bart.

Du Pré shrugged.

"All it take, one of them fuck up it all goes," said Du Pré. "They got at least an idea now, maybe they don't be such assholes, but even then some of these ranchers, pretty brushy, they don't like *anybody* mess with them."

"I like Agent Wallace," said Bart.

"Him pretty good," said Du Pré, "but that's just him. They got ten others east, twenty more north, and twenty here. All it takes, one of them piss off somebody. Our people, here, they are mighty hard to piss off. Oh, yes. Most of them, you know, you send them half a wrong look, you are very dead now."

"Foote calls this the hot rug treatment. You roll the rug out over everything and then wait, and see what scurries out the sides."

"They don't scurry, I think," said Du Pré. "I think maybe they dig them foxhole."

"Christ, I am tired," said Bart.

"October, it seems a long time ago," said Du Pré.

"It was a long time ago," said Bart. "We weren't old men last October. You know I have not thought one thing about anything but death. Sixteen of them, and then the two in the car accident. Nice, normal deaths, those were. Pleasant ones, you know. Just two drunk kids missed a turn."

"Who lives, both worlds?" said Du Pré.

"Eh?"

"That Corey Banning," said Du Pré, "she said that, we were talking, I wondered, you know, these people were shot cutting the fences that night, but Stemples, they come to me before and tell me about shot cattle, cut fence. And the St. Francis brothers. Then they are gone the night the two are killed, then the car is dumped, them in it, probably lowered down, the canner truck."

"If," said Bart.

"I never look at that ME's report on them two," said Du Pré.

"Neither did I," said Bart.

"What?"

"I don't remember that we ever got it," said Bart, "or if

161

we did I never saw it. Things were a bit hectic."

Bart went to the telephone. Du Pré went outside to smoke and look at the spring.

Pretty time, this is. But I can't see it.

Bart slammed out of the Sheriff's building, cursing.

"He sent it to Corey," said Bart, "and she promised to give us a copy right away, save the ME time and postage. She didn't, of course."

"Ah," said Du Pré. Corey, Corey, you weren't dead I'd yell at you.

"Anyway," said Bart, "they both died of gunshot wounds. But he could not fix a time of death, at all, because their bodies were refrigerated. Not frozen, just chilled, he thought. If they were kept at just above freezing, he couldn't give us any time, and so he didn't."

"Now them Stemple got no alibi," said Du Pré.

"They don't need one, at the moment," said Bart, "and Corey interviewed them over and over."

"Ah," said Du Pré. "Well, maybe this Harvey guy give us that file."

"I'll see," said Bart. "No, we'll both see. The ME was faxing us his report. Should be here. I'll be right out."

"Well," said Du Pré, "I bet you the woman was messed with and I bet you it was those fucking St. Francis brothers. And I bet you Corey was after poor Packy 'cause she knew he knew more'n he'd tell."

Bart went in and came right back out, holding papers.

"You care to drive, Mon Sewer?"

"OK."

"Well," said Bart, "I'm right. Now if Cousin Weasel Fat will share like a bighearted guy, which I am sure he is, we can maybe do something right for once. I haven't had so much experience of that in life, I am hungry for it."

Wallace was standing in the parking lot in front of the FBI trailers. He waved as they pulled in. Du Pré slowed to a crawl so he didn't splash mud on Wallace's suit.

"Good to see you," said Wallace. "And you won't believe it, but I was going to call this afternoon and apologize and explain that my predecessor failed to take you into her confidence. I really don't know why. We are a kinder, gentler FBI these days, to our brother officers. And if you believe that horseshit you deserve what you get."

"I goddamn know it is those St. Francis brothers," said Du Pré. "They kill those fool kids, stick them in the meat cooler they got, hide their car, dump it after they know about the others."

"No," said Bart, "the time doesn't work."

"It does if they are in jail and poor Packy is stuck with it," said Du Pré. "It work just fine. He brings the damn dog back, too."

Only person I am liking in all of this is the dog, thought Du Pré. Me included.

"She had that," said Wallace, "but she needed something more, and she was after it when Packy cracked and killed her. What, I don't know. But the St. Francis brothers are slobs and fools and we will be dropping in on them at about four this morning waving warrants. They're fuckups. I like fuckups. I can't catch the good ones, they make lists and like that. Dos and don'ts. First thing, you murder someone, don't overcomplicate it. Kill 'em, get rid of the weapon, answer all questions sort of, and you're ally ally oxen free."

"OK," said Bart. "Now, I don't give a rat's ass about us getting glorious arrests. I won't run for reelection. I don't care about even a bit of the credit. But I would sure like this not to turn into a war, you know, and peace I will have, whatever it takes."

Harvey Wallace looked at Bart for a long moment.

He grinned.

He stuck out his hand.

163

"How nice," he said, "that you'd like to avoid mass slaughter. Now, would you care to speculate as to just how many wholly illegal automatic weapons right on up to cannon there are out there? There's one P-thirty-eight, four fifty-caliber Brownings and a twenty-millimeter cannon, and two Mustangs. The late models, also with cannon. Where, I do not know. There's all sorts of soldiers, and this state produced an uncommon lot of Lurps and SEALS and demolitions champions. They don't like governments, cops, daytime TV, fluoride in their water, Democrats, big words, and especially they don't like arrogant pricks from Washington, D.C."

Bart laughed.

"But I will have these murderers. Because if we can't find them this is going to be a sport out here, like clubbing jackrabbits and shooting gophers of an idle Sunday. We can't have that, you will admit."

Bart and Du Pré nodded.

"Nobody around here's dumb enough to do anything with the St. Francis brothers. We bust them, dead end, right? My esteemed colleagues to the east and north will perhaps find out something about the vagaries of Montana, but not much else. The Martins need not talk. The folk to the north present a united front of silence."

"It's wrong," said Bart.

"What the fuck does that have to do with anything?" said Wallace. "Point is, no one did it for revenge or gain, it just sort of happened, other'n the St. Francis brothers, and so no one will speak. And there's nothing in it for them, anyway. You hate someone these days, give 'em a cow. Nobody wants the neighbor's ranch. Can't even hope for anyone to covet enough to drop a damn dime. Nope."

"I got a thought," said Du Pré. "Them two killed on the first night? We were wondering, maybe there is a Martin kid, some kid spying on these people, tipped the Martins off, said, well, these fools all plan to cut fences, this night."

"Good," said Wallace.

"Kid is maybe an environmentalist member, you know, even helps plan it."

"Excellent," said Wallace.

"You think of it?" said Du Pré.

"We did, and the little bitch is Angela Green, one Harold Green having married a Martin sister. Big wheeze in environmental lunacies. She calls home regularly, nothing much there."

"Young kid?"

"Twenty-three."

"You talk to her?"

"Oh, we talked to her a lot. See, she gives passionate speeches about running cattle off the public lands, bringing back the buffalo, and what pigs ranchers are. Good speaker, too. I've heard her a bunch of times."

"Her parents are not mad at her?"

"Parents love their kids, even unto Murder One and such," said Harvey. "Interesting, though, how she howls and yells about destroying them but she comes here in the summer to help out. The old homestead."

"What'd she say?" said Bart.

"Oh," said Wallace, "she said her business was hers and her parents' business was theirs and now please fuck off and get out of my face."

"Uh," said Du Pré. "She sounds a real Montana girl, her."

"Right down to her custom boots," said Wallace. "And we even got to the idiots who planned this spree of cattle shooting and fence cutting that got sixteen people killed. If you count the mourners the avalanche got and the bear ate."

Bart and Du Pré waited.

"She rigorously opposed that course of action and so

165

they went off to plan their suicides in more sympathetic surroundings."

"How would she know the date?" said Bart.

"She's a spectacularly beautiful woman," said Wallace.

"I see," said Bart.

✤ CHAPTER 31 ✤

I am sick worried, you," said Madelaine. "All this time you are getting thin, you don't smile, you smoke too much, there, you drink that whiskey, and you don't drink it for fun."

"I am sorry," said Du Pré. "This whole business, you know, the place I live blowing all apart, nothing will ever be the same now, you know. I don't see you, I don't see my daughter, grandchildren, all, I don't play the damn fiddle, I am not Du Pré anymore, you are right."

"Well," said Madelaine, "us Métis we are here, Montana, sure by 1700. That Lewis and Clark Expedition it come, we are here, we draw them map and give it to Blackfeet to give to them because we are Métis and if we give it then we are betrayers. So there has been lot of blood, you know. My great-great-great-grandfather was that Mitch Bouyer, he send the other Métis scouts away and he go down the hill, die with Custer. So it is not the first time and you are not God and you can't stop everything. I tell you you going to play that damn fiddle Susan's this afternoon for sure. Or I cry and cry and cry till you so miserable you cry, too. I do that, Du Pré. You are dying right in front of me, I will not let you."

"I feel pretty good," said Du Pré.

"Shit you feel pretty good. Your friends, enemies, neighbors, they are some of them murderers. You damn near die, avalanche, you know you toss in the night and sweat some. You lie there, I get towels, mop you off."

"Oh," said Du Pré.

"I already know you are a hero," said Madelaine. "I don't need to hear it more."

"OK," said Du Pré.

"I got your fiddle. I buy new strings for it. I put them on as good as I can. Now you tune it, you take your Madelaine, the bar, we have some drinks, I listen to you play, I even make you a nice red shirt, send away, one of them paisley scarves. You wear them, please. We go, have some good time, come back here, fuck, and you sleep."

Du Pré took a hot shower and he put on clean jeans and his new shirt and knotted his scarf and they drove down to the Toussaint Bar. He grabbed his old rawhide fiddle case with the porcupine-quill stars on it all worn away and he carried it in. There weren't any other cars there, odd for a Sunday afternoon.

Du Pré held the door open for Madelaine. He stepped inside. Fifty friends sat there silently. There was a big table all covered with food, a whole pig on a huge wooden platter, one his father Catfoot had carved from a big piece of basswood he had sent off for.

Cousin LeBlanc from Canada was there with his accordion.

Cousin Beauharne from North Dakota with his guitar and harmonica and his dancing shoes. He did the old Métis dances, old as the Romans.

Bunch of people, good people.

"You get that big drink, Du Pré," said Cousin LeBlanc, "then we play that good music."

Du Pré looked round, somewhat shocked. The Stemples

167

were there and the Moores and many other couples, some of them Du Pré thought might have had something to do with the murders. But they were here and they seemed happy.

If old Benetsee was here, I would like that, Du Pré thought, I need him very much now. What is in this that I cannot see, or don't want to? Who am I to decide this? What do I do, I don't know.

Play some music, my friends. Drink some whiskey and love my woman. Forget death for some time now and let some good things be remembered.

Du Pré felt a tug on his right sleeve. He looked over and there stood Benetsee, grinning, holding out a huge glass of whiskey and ice.

"You play them song, the voyageur," said Benetsee. "They go through that dark forest, they die in the black water, but they sing and fiddle there, Du Pré, you give me tobacco and you drink and fiddle."

Du Pré rolled them each a cigarette and lit them and he had a pull of whiskey and he put his arm on Benetsee's shoulders.

"Old man," he said, "I . . . we got to stop this now, you know, the women will have many tears and the children misfortunes. What do we do?"

"Good," said Benetsee.

"What good?"

"You always asking me what you to do, never us," said Benetsee. "Pretty dumb, you are."

"Hey!" said Cousin LeBlanc, "You tune that fiddle, yes, we play them paddle songs, pack carry songs, you know the one about the bet, carry them pack on the portage?"

I grow up to I'm three I know it, Du Pré thought, how many hundred-pound packs the voyageur carry, huh? Three, sometimes four, but this song they say they carry ten, half a ton, roll home on their balls, I guess.

The strong portageur.

Du Pré pulled on the new strings to stretch them, ran the blob of rosin over the finger lengths. He tuned, sending the strings far sharp and letting them down to pitch.

Cousin Beauharne began to pick bass lines, Cousin Le-Blanc let the bellows out, Du Pré fiddled. A young couple, Métis, Du Pré didn't know them, got out on the floor and began to dance, heel and toe, the old tapping.

We do that, the buffalo robes pegged on the ground. The decks of the little ships bring us first here, some say we were in that Gulf of St. Lawrence by 1200, maybe. Running from them damn priests and tax gatherers. Lot of cabin foundations all over the north Rockies go so far back the Cheyennes, they was still in Iowa raising pumpkins and corn.

Pretty old music, pretty old blood.

I go to Brittany sometime.

The song ended. LeBlanc and Beauharne looked at Du Pré. Gabriel drew one long note out of his fiddle and then he started a lament, one the voyageurs sang, about the women they had left behind who weren't pulling on the rope to help them back; they were sparking with the soldiers who never left the fort.

Maybe even not building them canoe so tight for their voyageurs, so that the canoe come apart, the Big Rapids, the voyageurs they drown. All the voyageur hearts in a big brass kettle, lost at the foot of the rapids, their souls like smoke underwater, forever reaching for and never rising to the light.

Pretty tough times.

More people got out on the dance floor. The young couple put arms across the shoulders of others who wanted to learn and taught them the steps quarter-time. Everybody laughed, everybody danced.

Du Pré looked up to see Jacqueline and Raymond come

in. His daughter pregnant again, this would be the last, though, the doctor said. It would be twelve. She had two sets of twins.

But she laughed and she danced with her Raymond and Du Pré felt very proud, he looked at her and played one song just for her and everyone else stopped dancing but Raymond and Jacqueline.

Du Pré was running sweat. He stopped and wiped his face and set his fiddle down. LeBlanc and Beauharne went on, moving the tempo up a little every third bar. The choruses rounded and backed together.

Du Pré made his way to the bar. Madelaine was sitting on a stool, smiling like a June bride.

"It is my Du Pré," she said, "my Gabriel, not the old grouch, always mumbling, himself. Ah. You have not forgot to play that fiddle. Give my Du Pré a good red shirt and some whiskey and he will play that fiddle, hah."

Du Pré grinned. He looked down the bar and saw Bart behind it, pulling beers and mixing drinks. Harvey Wallace was at the far end, wearing jeans and boots today, smiling.

Du Pré had some whiskey and a cigarette.

He went back up to the bandstand and he picked up his fiddle and he fiddled a fisher's jig. The Métis were great fishermen. Pull them pike up, split them and smoke them, get them salmon and them big trout.

LeBlanc and Beauharne put down their instruments.

Old Benetsee shuffled up to the stage and he sat down on the front of it and he pulled a fresh-made willow flute from his jacket and he blew into it softly for a few moments, his gnarled old fingers seeking out the holes.

He played. It was a tune like no other that Du Pré had ever heard, the scale strange, the rhythm deep and turning round and the notes soft and piercing all at once.

The old man's face was shadowed underneath his stained old hat. The red willow stem stuck down. His fin-

gers rose and clamped again and the crowd sat silent, trans-
fixed, breathing softly if at all.

I have never heard this old man do this, Du Pré thought,
how much else is buried deep within him? I don't even
know how old he is.

I do not know.

He has sometimes made me very angry.

I might as well be angry at the Red River.

Shadows or the ghosts of buffalo.

Old blood.

Help me.

✤ CHAPTER 32 ✤

We just flat may never know at all," said Bart.

Harvey Wallace sipped his coffee and he blew
out a long stream of blue smoke from his mouth. He set his
pipe down in the ashtray.

"Could be," he said, "but you put enough glue around,
your fly steps in it. Except for one thing. This isn't a crime
done by just one person for just one reason. Those fool kids
came out here and stepped right down into the crack between the old time and the new. Angela Green keeps
making speeches damning what her family's done for six
generations, and they still send her three grand a month. So
go figure. I can't indict indulgent parents."

"Is it really true that that fool Governor had a bear killed
over west of Glacier? Flown here and dumped so he could
claim the bear that ate the folks killed in the avalanche had
been killed?"

"I don't even need to check," said Harvey Wallace. "It's true. I know in my bones. I know in my dick. I know it better than my own name. I have worked in government service lo these many years and I tell you this is true."

"Yah," said Du Pré, "that Old Black Claws he is gone, sure. I miss him, he used to come round, I am up there, see who I am. A gentleman. Other'n he eat ol' Jimmy Moore's big dray horse that one time."

"Huh?" said Bart.

"You were . . . uh . . . not here," said Du Pré. "When them grizzly are all protected, the federal government, one time, Old Black Claws he is much hungry, he come down in the late spring, climb the fence, old Moore's horse pasture, drive his big Percheron stud into the corner, break his neck, one swipe of his paw."

Du Pré took a drag of his smoke.

"Old Jimmy, he is looking out the window, he see this, he cuss some awful, pull on his boots, go to get his rifle, shoot that bear. Jimmy's wife, she say, no, you can't shoot that bear, big trouble, put you in jail. You call them Fish and Game."

"Hoo boy," said Harvey Wallace.

"So Jimmy he does and they are not there, phone ring, finally he get some kid who say, 'Are you sure it is a grizzly?'

"Jimmy, he say yes, he know what a grizzly is. Kid says, 'You sure it kill your horse? Your horse didn't just die, that bear eating it, helping clean up?'

"Jimmy, he say a bunch of things before he tear the phone out of the wall and then he get his gun but by then Old Black Claws, he has dragged the stud horse through the fence and up the canyon and so Jimmy he just shrug and say, 'Well, I guess that old bastard was hungry.' "

"Jesus," said Bart.

"Yeah," said Harvey Wallace, "kid must have watched

that dumb TV show, the one with the bear eats soybeans or something."

"But why," said Bart, "would Black Claws just up and leave? Benetsee said he went north? So, how'd he get the idea?"

Du Pré shrugged. He didn't want to talk about it.

Booger Tom stomped through the front door and back through the living room to the kitchen where the three younger men were sitting.

"Goddamn lawn forcement," he said. "Ever' time I turn round there's another one a ya spoilsports. When do the preachers start stampedin' in? The company around here gets lower and lower."

"We were talking about lynching someone, for the practice," said Bart. "Watch your damn mouth."

"Any a you geniuses figger out who done all of this yet?" said Booger Tom. "Or I got to do that for you, too?"

The phone rang. Bart picked it up, listened, hung up after saying only "Christ, yeah, right there."

"What?" said Harvey.

"Oh, one of my good upstanding local citizens is holed up in his machine shed, armed to the teeth, while two of your guys, Harvey, are crouched behind their car pointing guns at the guy in the shed while he points a gun at them. Mexican standoff, but I think we had better haul ass."

"Who?" said Harvey. "What are my guys doing there, anyway?"

"Asking questions," said Bart, moving for the door.

"That does it," said Harvey. "I'll just have them mail out questionnaires from now on, prepared confessions."

Du Pré laughed.

"My guys won't shoot unless they get shot at," said Harvey.

"Not comforting," said Bart.

"Where are they?" said Du Pré.

"Well," said Bart, "Benny Klein is in his machine shed and the two FBI guys are behind their car. Susan is in the house, watching. She's so pissed I think when the FBI guys leave Benny will stay barricaded in there anyway."

Du Pré drove them rapidly toward Benny's. It wasn't that far. He turned in the driveway and saw the light blue government motor-pool car and the two agents crouched behind it.

Bart and Harvey got out and sauntered up to the agents.

"Benny!" Bart yelled. "Cut the crap and come on out. Jesus Christ, man, what the fuck are you doing?"

"I wanna be on *Sixty Minutes*," said Benny. He emerged from the shed in a filthy coverall, carrying a steel box wrench. "They hollered, I come out of the shed here with my Magnum *wrench* in hand, and they go for their guns and I dive back in the shop and here I am. Wanna have me tighten down your fucking gaskets, you morons?" He glared at the agents, who looked at the ground.

"Magnum what?" said Bart.

"The box wrench," said Benny. "Look, I don't blame them. Everybody here is wound about nine cranks too tight, you know. Susan is in the house there, probably got a bead drawn on their heads."

"Yes!" said Susan, from behind the paint shed, fifteen feet from the government car. She stepped out, carrying a pump sawed-off shotgun.

"I think that I go down the bar, have a drink," said Du Pré. "You know it is pretty bad when the former Sheriff and his wife, they are about to declare war on the U.S. government."

"Former Sheriff," sighed Harvey Wallace.

"Damn it," said one of the agents, "it was all a mistake. I saw the flash of metal and I dove."

"I'm sorry," said Benny. "I wasn't thinking how scared you are of wrenches. All this is going to lead to is some more folks getting killed, Bart. Nobody's gonna get nowhere but us who lives here. Nowhere."

"OK, guys," said Harvey Wallace, "go pull in your fellow agents. Pack it in, head for Billings, do it right now. I'll call you later. Don't even go back to check and see the door's latched."

"Suits me," said the other agent. "This is bullshit."

They drove off.

"My job just showed the first signs of creeping death," said Harvey Wallace. "I now have to tell my superiors that our best course of action is to leave. They will not like it, but it is so."

"I'm sorry," said Bart.

"I, uh, never learned that the toes you step on today may be connected to the ass you need to kiss tomorrow," said Harvey. "And I believe that you have a means of getting to the Attorney General of the United States. Bart? It is a matter of life and death."

"I'll call lawyer Charles Foote," said Bart. "Tell him either get you guys out of here or he has to come here himself."

"He hates it that much?" said Harvey.

"He likes to say so," said Bart. He walked off with his telephone.

"Get them all out of here, I hope," said Du Pré. "I think sometime the whole air gone crazy, all you got to do is breathe it and you are nuts."

"That kind of time," said Harvey.

"Angela Green," said Du Pré.

"Only hope," said Harvey, "you get that little girl to sing a nice clear song and we are someplace. Not, forget it. It's the Martins and their allies, whoever, a few rich ranchers to the north. You know how I know that? Poor folks make threats; rich folks do things and smile. That's all, folks."

Poor folks act like people, rich folks act like governments, thought Du Pré. Damn, I thought that my own self.

"She ain't in my jurisdiction," said Bart, "and I think the next Sheriff over is in on all this, anyway."

"Probably," said Harvey.

"Christ," said Bart.

"Yeah," said Harvey, "this is a dog, sure enough. All kinds of leads but they don't go anywhere. Funny thing about conspiracies like this, what with our system of civil liberties and proof beyond a reasonable doubt, it's almost impossible to break one of 'em."

"What about the Mafia?" said Du Pré.

"Idiots," said Harvey. "They'd make more money driving trucks."

"Angela Green," said Bart.

"All you got," said Harvey.

"What exactly *have* you got?" said Bart.

"Come look at it," said Harvey, "but you just never tell anyone I let you peek at it."

✤ CHAPTER 33 ✤

I am needing your help, old man," yelled Du Pré.

He sat down and waited for the old man to come.

Some shit, this, I don't believe, me, one minute that Harvey Weasel Fat gone away all nice. But Benetsee say that the killing is all through, there will be no more. I don't understand what he mean, I never have till later. What he say only make sense looking back.

I want to maybe ride horses with my Madelaine, go up in the Wolf Mountains, see maybe my grandfather's ghost, find some place there is a tree that shouldn't grow there. Look at them old mine, where someone hoped till their money it was all gone. That little place high up on Toussaint Peak, where the turquoise lies all around, chunks of it, some dark green, some blue, some almost white.

I wonder what just shoved them Wolf Mountains right up out of the plains, it is down there, though. Got very big shoulders, it.

I dream now, I am out in the snow forever on a piss-flat plain, me a little black thing struggling through the deep snow toward the horizon, flat white line, not even any damn wind, just me and nothing at all.

Maybe this is why them voyageur songs, they are all mostly sad. The ones for dancing with your women, they are not sad, but the others they are, long haul in the canoe for the Here Before Christ, them Hudson's Bay Company bastards.

Long time, much blood, we fight a war there, Selkirk Colony, we fight a war here now, and there is sadness. All them people dead and their parents crying for them and they don't understand.

Me, my Jacqueline, my Maria, Madelaine, they are dead I will not understand either.

Some shit, this.

Them damn dead fools they stay home they be alive and still be fools.

Piss me off. All of it.

Got good reasons break the law, it is still a broken law.

Du Pré wandered back to his Rover, fished around under the seat, pulled out a fifth of whiskey. He had a slug and looked up at the Wolfs, the snow on the peaks. The wind had changed and it was blowing down from them, thick with fresh pine.

I dream of flowers growing out of the eye pits of skulls, I dream of bears under the ice and snow, I dream of wolf cubs stolen and raised in cages, far from the north where they are free.

I dream of young fools knowing for a few seconds maybe how little time they had to live.

They would have been surprised. They would not have believed it.

Us people we do not believe in death. That is something, it happen to other people.

He rolled a cigarette. Far off down the road there was the jangling whine of a VW engine. It came closer. It slowed.

An old VW bus, painted with ordinary house paint, the usual peace symbols and slogans.

A long-haired young man got out. He waved limply to Du Pré and he walked up the drive to the Rover, round it, and he walked up to Du Pré and around him and on to the porch and he banged hard on the old door.

Du Pré looked off at the middle distance.

"Hey, man," the longhair said, "you know where the shaman is?"

"At the dentist's," said Du Pré, "get a tooth pulled."

"Oh," said the longhair. "Who are you?"

"I'm the other shaman," said Du Pré. "My teeth, they are all right."

"Oh, yeah, cool," said the longhair. "Lissen, I want to go on a vision quest, you dig, and I wanted to see the shaman, you know."

"Oh, yes," said Du Pré.

"This is Benjamin Medicine Eagle's place, right?"

"Oh, yes," said Du Pré, "but he is not here. I maybe can help you."

"Cool," said the longhair. "I mean, I don't know where

the fucking butte is, man, where I got to go for the vision."

"It is up that canyon," said Du Pré, pointing up toward a cut in the flanks of the Wolfs. "Not very big."

Big thunderstorm coming in, just hit the mountains, though, thought Du Pré, big one, hit maybe two hours.

It was a nice warm day.

"Listen," said Du Pré, pulling up a handful of dried fallow grass, "you take this up that canyon, you see a little butte right ahead of you, you get on top and light this sweet grass, very holy grass, lie down, wait there. Maybe all night, next day, next night, too."

"Yeah," said the longhair, "I know it's tough. I seen *Dances with Wolves* ten times, you know."

"Oh, yes," said Du Pré. He had laughed so hard at the wrong times that the manager of the theater in Billings threw him out.

Good thing, too, me, I don't sometime like them Sioux, but that movie, pretty insulting, you know. Make them look like a bunch of idiots, no blood to them either.

"You can't wear no white-man stuff," said Du Pré, "no blankets. You got any furs, your truck there?"

"Furs are cruel," said the longhair.

"Well," said Du Pré, "I give you my blessing. You got to hurry now, you know, you aren't there before the sun is off that peak there, you got to wait till tomorrow."

"Thanks, man!" said the longhair.

He drove off and Du Pré watched the VW turn and go up the Forest Service road. He went to his Rover and got his binoculars and he watched the longhair take off all his clothes and then put on his shoes and walk up the trail toward the little butte stuck in the throat of the canyon.

Good place, that top of that butte. Thunderstorm hit, it is always hit by lightning, it is scorched and burnt up there, the rock.

The clouds were bunching black and rising above the

Wolfs. They flashed inside, dark purple in the black.

Oh, I am a prick, Du Pré thought, but I was drove to it.

Du Pré had another draw on the bottle of whiskey.

I am never see my Madelaine, I don't see my daughter, I have not talked to my other daughter in weeks, I am losing all my life I care for.

What do I do?

Bart, me, we can't quit. We are not going to find out nothing we can use and that Harvey Weasel Fat, he can piss up a rope, stand under it while it dries, you know.

A whistle.

Falcon whistle. Prairie falcon, hunting, hunting.

Poor Corey Banning, she dive so fast she hit the rock.

What?

I need this old man now, tell me what to do. If he know. Not always he does know, maybe just them riddles.

Old Black Claws, he gone north.

Shit.

Du Pré heard some thunder, distant, deep. He walked to where he could see the whole of the Wolfs stretched out east to west, rising from the red and yellow plains. Island in the sky, there.

The clouds sent a lash of black rain down; lightning stitched the canyons, struck along the ridges.

Been up on them a couple times, that hit, the rocks blow up like grenades. Five-hundred-pound grenades.

Some movement up that little canyon.

Du Pré put the binoculars to his eyes.

The naked longhair was running flat-out down the trail toward his VW. A young grizzly was chasing him, maybe two hundred yards behind, so the bear was just having a little fun.

I call you Young Black Claws, thought Du Pré, this is very good, I am feeling some better now.

A grip on his elbow.

"Eh?" said Benetsee. "You got nothing better to do, tease some poor white fool like that? He wants to be Indian. I don't know why anybody wants be something else. What's the use? You got me wine?"

Du Pré nodded. He handed the old man his tobacco pouch and he went to the Rover and fished out a gallon jug of horrible cheap fizzy wine and he brought it back and picked up a jar out of the grass and shook out the beetles in it and he filled it and gave it to Benetsee.

The old man drained it.

He put his cigarette in his mouth and waited for Du Pré to light it.

The VW screamed past.

"Funny times," said Benetsee.

"No shit," said Du Pré. "Me, I am not laughing so much."

"This land, pretty quiet for a long time. It be quiet again," said Benetsee. "Don't do it by your time, though. You wait."

"OK," said Du Pré. "But I can't see myself no more, you know."

"OK," said Benetsee. "I wonder when you ask. You got questions."

Du Pré nodded.

"Go sleep, your grandfathers."

"They are in the little cemetery, Toussaint," said Du Pré.

"They got their holes," said Benetsee. "You go, take your blanket, you know. Give some tobacco, little sweet grass, say a prayer with that Father Van Den Heuvel, he is good man."

"OK," said Du Pré.

"OK?" said Benetsee.

✤ CHAPTER 34 ✤

Ah," said Madelaine, "well, I am maybe having some hope of seeing my Du Pré maybe. I have not, nearly a year now, you know. I see . . . well, I go pray. You see your grandfathers, you say hello, your Madelaine maybe not let you back in the house some soon day."

Du Pré nodded. The jukebox was blaring and a couple of people were playing pool at Susan's. Not much else. It was an early June night warm with crickets and the scent of the tangled little roses that grew in the little draws near the water.

That Custer, his men, that is the smell they die in, that and dust, the Little Bighorn, Du Pré thought. What a dumb man, him. That Mitch Bouyer, he die with Custer. Us Métis, we die a lot, white-man quarrels, die a lot, Indian quarrels, weren't for all them sonsofbitches we live a long goddamn time, you bet.

The door opened and Harvey Wallace padded in. He wore running shoes and old clothes and a windbreaker to hide his gun.

Ol' Harvey Weasel Fat, I am think he could paint his face I'd feel better, thought Du Pré, them Blackfeet chase you clear home. Then they wait. Chew on a little jerky. Lie in the river, breathe through a reed. Lie by the horses, covered in grass, you walk over them up them come, stab you, left thigh inside high, slash the artery, you whirl, right wrist, then your throat.

Who told me all this? I don't know.

Harvey sat down with them, a soda in his hand.

"Madelaine," he said, "how are you this fine evening? You want to dance maybe?" He spoke good Coyote French, too.

Madelaine smiled and she got up and they danced by the jukebox.

Du Pré watched, sipped his drink.

Good woman. I am such a pain in the ass, big one, lately, maybe she take up with Harvey Weasel Fat. No, she like me OK. She is just worried some.

Du Pré went to the bar, got another drink, another pink wine for Madelaine.

Harvey and Madelaine came back to the table. She sat down and had a drink of her pink wine. Harvey stood and drained his soda.

"I been a cop worse places," said Harvey.

"There are lots of them," said Du Pré. "You know, Harvey, I don't think some that we ever find out sometimes. That Bart, he is a madman, do his job good, all of it. We ask and ask but no one here say anything. Nobody is bragging. Nobody."

"Yeah," said Harvey, "well, I like to fish. Sometimes I won't even bait the hook, you know, I like to fish so much, not be disturbed."

Du Pré nodded.

"That evening rise is starting," said Harvey, "and I am going to fish on the bottom. You know, I talked to poor Packy's wife and I don't think now Packy had anything to do with anything. Just a short fuse and poor Corey lit it. Ya never know. Guy just snapped."

Du Pré nodded.

Yah, well, Packy he do whatever his sweet government tell him, he get scared, he stop it some for just a little while. Too bad, he was pretty good guy and he got kids, wife, all left and no money. I got to talk to Bart about that.

183

Susan and Benny came out of the back with plates. They sat at the table next to Du Pré and Madelaine, to eat dinner early before the rush started, if it ever did. When the nights were so short and the days long and the light hung in the west until nearly eleven at night the bar did a slender business.

"'Lo, Harvey," said Susan. "You want something?"

"No, no," said Harvey, "you eat. If someone comes in I'll get them whatever."

Susan nodded. She had a forkful of meatloaf, the night's special.

"Harvey," said Benny, "you don't hit seventeen, you play the dealer."

Harvey nodded.

Du Pré sipped his drink, rolled a smoke. He lit it, lit Madelaine's filter tip. They smoked and held hands.

"That a message?" said Harvey.

"Line from a song I like," said Benny. "I just hope things go better now. This is awful."

"What song?" said Harvey.

"I dunno what the title is," said Benny, "but the song is about how fast them summer wages go, you know."

"Ah," said Harvey, "yeah, now I remember. I like that song, too."

"You get your fiddle, Du Pré," said Madelaine.

Du Pré went out and got it and he came back and he played it very softly while the cigarette smoke rose to the ceiling. No one came into the bar.

He played the old laments, the songs of tiredness and loneliness in the black-green forests the voyageurs paddled through, far to the north where their canoes crossed the footprints of glaciers and the rising land. Four feet a century, in a flat place the rivers ran one way for a while and then another.

The Red River of the North was mostly lakes.

Harvey left. Benny and Susan held hands, Madelaine rubbed Du Pré's knee.

They all left the bar at two in the morning. Susan never closed it early, saying that a reliable place to get a drink was a must in a small town.

Du Pré dropped Madelaine off and he drove the little ways to the Catholic cemetery out behind the little church, in its groves of Russian olives. The place was well kept, plastic flowers on some of the graves and the weeds pulled and piled in one spot for burning in the fall.

An owl hooted softly.

Great horned he is hunting. The Hush Wing. Maybe another Hush Wing, they don't care, they just eat.

Du Pré pulled his bedroll out of the truck and he carried it and his whiskey and he walked into the cemetery and he went to the place where his grandparents and parents were buried, his wife near them, too. He unrolled the blankets pinned in their canvas cover and he sat cross-legged and he looked up at the Dipper, rolling around the polestar.

The sky was clear and the stars burned fiercely, hanging low.

Light my cigarette, one of them.

He drank.

A bullbat shot past overhead. He heard them call, and then gone.

Sweet sound, them goatsuckers.

Du Pré thought of Black Claws, under the snow.

Almost get me to eat. Well, I been killed almost, bunch of times.

Pretty stars.

A coyote howled, the choirmaster.

The chorus joined him.

God's dogs, they must know everything that is important. Very smart, them coyote, too smart, they get into trouble being so smart. Good way to trap them set two traps, one where they look at it, the other where they go to think about it, a little rise nearby.

The coyotes stopped. Then a yipping.

Got a rabbit, they run that rabbit in shifts till it is worn out. Poor old jackrabbit, he don't got a thing but speed.

But they don't run, can the coyote find them?

I do all the thinking good as I can and I don't got dick. All I got is Madelaine pissed off and my friend Bart a badge he don't really want and the same shit start again soon, the summer is here.

So where am I.

Sleeping with my grandfathers in the cemetery, my father he is there, my mother, my wife. Lot of my aunts, great-aunts, friends, old people I knew as a kid, I wish that they were here, I was not old or smart enough to ask them the right questions and they knew many things, old people always do. I thought that I would when I got older but it does not seem so.

Du Pré drank.

He looked up. The Dipper had moved round another hour. Good clock, it was.

No coyotes. They are eating rabbit.

Owl eating owl.

Me, I am drinking whiskey and smoking that Bull Durham.

Wondering what the fuck I am thinking of, doing what I am doing.

Nobody else dumb enough to.

Angela Green. I talk to her.

We don't know *nothing*.

That Taylor Martin, he spit in our faces.

Du Pré fell back on his bedroll. The night was cold and the dew forming.

He crawled into his bedroll and smoked one last cigarette.

He stubbed it out, put his face in the soogans, and slept.

He woke up just before dawn when the birds began to chirp and sing, the night hunters passed, and the day hunters passed by, in the air or on the ground.

The wind brought a scent of fox piss.

Du Pré sat up. He rolled a smoke. He looked up at the Wolf Mountains.

"OK," he said.

"Thank you, grandfathers."

✦ CHAPTER 35 ✦

W ell," said Benny Klein, "I guess that they thought if they held this hearing near us they'd never make it out alive."

Du Pré nodded.

The Fish and Wildlife people were dropping another batch of wolves into the Wolf Mountains, but they didn't want to announce that anywhere near the Wolf Mountains.

"Yeah," said Du Pré, "well, maybe they pitch these wolves out of an airplane, parachutes on them."

The hearing was being held on the campus of Northern Montana College in a room in the library. Most of the ranchers who had come were wearing cowshit-covered boots and occupying themselves with grinding it into the rug.

"Will they ever learn?" said Benny.

Du Pré shook his head.

"I know people like this, the army," said Du Pré. "Someone tell them that Chinese women are built sideways, they believe it, rest of their life. It is not much good, this talk.''

Du Pré looked round the room. He saw the young woman who had been so angry with him at the last hearing. Seemed like ten years ago.

She saw Du Pré and glared at him. She nudged another young woman near her and pointed.

The two looked hard at Du Pré.

''I don't know who that one on the right is,'' said Du Pré, ''but the one on the left is that Angela Green. You look at her good, Benny, she is the only way we find anything out, you bet.''

Angela was tall, dark-haired, and pale-eyed. She bent to whisper in her companion's ear and then they both sat down.

One of the Fish and Wildlife reps called the meeting to order, said it was open to public commentary, looked at the list in her hand, called a name, and sat down looking bored.

The decision had been made long ago. The hearing was a sop.

A rancher rose and walked to the witness stand, while most of the wolf crowd tittered.

The man spoke haltingly, shyly. He said that he saw no reason to return wolves, that they would kill stock, and that he was opposed to it. Montana was not a park.

He left the stand, walking slowly, dragging his left leg; it was an artificial one.

Which war you lose that in? Du Pré thought. Korea, that is it, I know that guy, he has the place just over the line. Bill Gustaffson, he is the brand inspector there.

Du Pré went out to smoke. There were a couple ranchers outside, too, having cigarettes. They nodded at Du Pré.

''This year the wolf bullshit,'' said one. ''Then next year they'll raise the grazing fees and we'll be out of business.''

"Aw, Wally," said the other, "we can open a tofu stand for the little bastards. We'll love it."

Wally shrugged.

Du Pré finished his cigarette and went back in.

Another rancher got off the stand.

Angela Green rose and she made her way gracefully up to the stand, and she began to speak in a low voice, pleading for the return of the predator to the ecosystem. It was meant to be. So much damage had been done, by her family, for one, and this was some way to put it right. The wolf was the symbol of wilderness. Why, in Minnesota wolves killed hardly any cattle at all. The objections of the ranchers were foolish.

She went on until the F and W rep stopped her for speaking longer than the allowed minutes.

She walked past Du Pré on her way outside, a leather cigarette case in her hand, the kind that has a lighter in it.

Du Pré followed.

They smoked on opposite sides of the walkway, each leaning up against a railing.

Du Pré looked at her. The new Levi's—old faded ones were for dudes. The custom boots, scuffed and resoled and heeled. The turquoise and silver buckle, an old one, sandcast and soldered.

Her hands they are the hands of a horsewoman, Du Pré thought, they are big, they grew big because she worked with them when she was a girl. She is very hard.

She leaned up against the railing in a way people do when they've leaned against a lot of fences.

She locked eyes with Du Pré.

"Long ways from the county," she said pleasantly.

"Uh," said Du Pré, "well, this is what start it all last time, you know, I am looking for things."

"I'm sure you are," she said.

"You like them wolf," said Du Pré.

"Magnificent animals," she said. "Think of this beautiful country. The buffalo, the Plains Indians, the elk on the river hills, the Eden that it was."

Yeah, Du Pré thought, well, this West not a very wild place till the white man come with guns, but look at the world now. Everybody got guns they try to kill each other, you bet.

"How long your people been here?" said Du Pré.

"One and one-quarter centuries," said Angela Green. "Busy raping the land." She walked over to Du Pré. She dropped her cigarette on the sidewalk and she ground it out with her boot.

"Taylor Martin was much man and my favorite uncle," she said.

Du Pré nodded. He drew on his smoke.

"I suppose we'll see each other often," said Angela, "and if you will excuse me now, I must go fight the good fight."

She kissed Du Pré on the cheek and she walked back through the door.

OK, Du Pré thought, I am seeing now. Not too much to do now. Oh, no, that Harvey Weasel Fat, he will *like* this, though. Plenty Indian enough, he always like a good joke.

Even if it is killing you, if it is doing it in a funny way, you got to laugh, this earth is that sort of place.

That Angela, she wouldn't crack, not ever.

But this can't happen again.

Benny wandered out.

"Buncha assholes singing three-part harmony in there," he said. "Are we here for a reason? I mean, I ain't even a deputy. Not anymore."

"Just spend some time," said Du Pré. "But there is no reason, not anymore, no."

They got into Du Pré's Rover and turned around and drove off. Du Pré stopped at a package store and got a fifth of whiskey and some sodas and some cheese and lunch meat.

Pack of Pall Malls. They were weak, but the best next to his hand-rolled ones.

He and Benny drove and drank and drove and drank.

"Am I still a sworn officer of the law?" said Benny.

"Oh, yeah," said Du Pré. "It is like a tattoo."

Benny nodded.

Du Pré was doing a hundred and ten down a two-lane blacktop.

"We are breaking a bunch of laws."

"Four," said Du Pré. "I am drunk more than the limit, we are on duty more or less, car is full of guns, all loaded, and I am driving fifty-five miles over the speed limit."

"Oh," said Benny, "is that all."

They shot past a Highway Patrolman. The patrol car roared after them, lights flashing.

Du Pré switched on his light bar and radio.

"Officer Du Pré," said Du Pré into the microphone, "taking a heart for transplant to the airport."

Crackle crackle.

The patrol car dropped behind.

"Dirty, dirty," said Benny.

"Pret' good whiskey," said Du Pré. "Have some."

Benny did.

"So what do we do now?" said Benny. "You know those feds are going batshit but they can't get anywhere. They got nothing and no one to frame even."

Du Pré nodded.

"You talk to Angela Green?" said Benny.

"Oh, yes," said Du Pré.

"What's she like?"

"Oh," said Du Pré, "dumb kid, you know, how they fight their parents. She will get knocked up next, I guess maybe."

191

Benny nodded.

"Pretty rich family."

"If they release the wolves again this'll happen again," said Benny.

"Yah."

"What are we gonna do?"

"We got to stop them," said Du Pré.

"How?"

"Well," said Du Pré, "I will have to think about that."

♣ CHAPTER 36 ♣

Dicked," said Harvey Wallace, aka Weasel Fat, "dicked, dicked, and dicked. I told 'em, we go there, we get dicked. No other way. Won't help my career."

"Uh," said Du Pré, "well, you don't know how to do nothing else, maybe?"

"I don't like doing nothing else," said Harvey. "I like chasing bad guys and running them down and throwing them in the slammer. I like to hunt ducks even more, come to think on it. I could be a duck cop."

"OK," said Du Pré, "now, you can come long as you behave, there, it is very important, you know, you do this, I don't want no more people killed here. Maybe this is not the best idea anybody ever had but I cannot, you know, think of any better one, I am too old and dumb."

"OK," said Harvey.

"I ask you to please do this," said Du Pré. "You don't dick me."

"OK," said Harvey Weasel Fat. "Sure as my name ain't

really Wallace I will not dick you. I drive you there and sit outside and I wait."

"Well," said Du Pré, "they will not, you know, come apart. We got no bullet. Gun it was fired from, guns, they are cut apart and melted down. Nobody knows nothing more than they got to. Smaller number of people in it than we thought. So there we are."

"Dicked," said Harvey.

"Dicked dicked dicked," said Madelaine. She stood in the kitchen doorway, hands on her hips, looking at Du Pré and Harvey, eyes narrowed. "You guys so dumb all you do is talk dirty, my house. I don't care you talk dirty, you be funny, though."

"OK," said Harvey.

"OK," said Du Pré. They were waiting on dinner. Being good boys.

"And you Harvey," said Madelaine, "you say dicked dicked dicked you know what you are sounding like?"

"No," said Harvey.

"You are whining," said Madelaine. "And you don't stop I call you Weasel Dick for couple weeks, see how you like that."

Harvey nodded. He looked sheepish.

Madelaine brought in the rest of the bowls and they sat down to supper. Her children wouldn't eat for an hour, but Du Pré and Harvey had other business.

Pot roast, potatoes, home-canned green beans, home-baked bread, and blackberry pie.

"Wonderful," said Harvey. "You let me wash dishes?"

"No," said Madelaine, "I don't want you guys around, you go do what you are going to do, come back, tell me, we go have some nice drinks. I listen better, your whining, I am about drunk."

"Me, Du Pré," said Harvey, "we give up our badges, we send you."

"Me," said Madelaine, "I am a woman. Dumb jobs like that, we send you guys. No way. Eat your pot roast."

"You speak pret' good Coyote French there, Harvey," said Du Pré.

"You damn Métis everywhere," said Harvey, "like ass pains and bad debts."

They finished and got up.

Madelaine kissed Du Pré. After a moment, she kissed Harvey on the cheek.

"You be back here, ten o'clock," said Madelaine.

"Maybe," said Du Pré. "I don't know."

"I know," said Madelaine. "I know what you are goin' do, too. Fine. Good idea. Be back by ten. I will want some pink wine then."

Du Pré and Harvey walked out to Harvey's government car and they got in and they drove off toward the Grange Hall fifty miles away. The building sat in the middle of the plains, miles from anything, and the Stockgrowers' Association was meeting there.

"What you got, the medicine bundle?" said Harvey.

Du Pré looked at the case in the back seat, a case made more than a century before for a double-recurve bone and Osage Orange bow. Du Pré wasn't sure where it had come from. Benetsee had given him the soft leather case, quilled and beaded and faded and cracked.

"Sacred shit," said Du Pré. "Don't think so very much, Harvey."

"OK," said Harvey.

Du Pré pulled a pint of whiskey out of his pocket and he had a drink and offered it to Harvey. Harvey shook his head.

"Afterward," said Harvey, "fine. I dunno what you got in mind, none of my business, but afterward."

Du Pré nodded. They turned onto the highway and shot hard for the east. The tires whined and birds burst up from crushed gopher carcasses mashed to the asphalt.

The sun was hot. They drove with the windows down. The blackbirds in the barrow pits chirred liquidly.

Du Pré looked to his left. He couldn't see the Wolfs, only the hayfields just past the fence. A red fox flamed in the green grass.

Du Pré rolled a smoke and lit it and he looked down to the south toward the far Missouri and the breaks, out over the buffalo country, where the cattle grazed so far from plates and tables. People back in there, too, in their Sears, Roebuck ranch houses, with the Siberian elms screening the wind, the windmills screaking overhead.

You can take this land but it makes you its own, he thought, got to be here some, it gets into your blood and bone and marrow and the dust colors your bones gold.

My country, this.

They made good time. Du Pré pointed off to the right, at the old Grange Hall red in the leafing cottonwoods. The ground around it was thick with cars and trucks, people moving slowly to the hall.

Harvey drove to the last row nearest the road and he switched off the engine and he sighed.

"I'll just wait here, like you asked," he said, "but don't kill anyone."

"Too much of that," said Du Pré.

Harvey nodded.

The last few of the ranchers were filing inside.

Du Pré got out. He opened the back door and took out the medicine bundle and he tucked it under his arm and he walked up to the door and he waited just a moment and then he walked inside.

People were talking and joshing and standing and sitting.

The Martins and some of their kin looked at Du Pré for a moment and then they went back to their conversations.

Clark Martin left his knot of family and he walked to the podium and he rapped on it with a stick of kindling. Everyone sat down but Du Pré. He leaned against the back wall.

"I call this meeting to order," Clark Martin said, loudly.

Du Pré slipped the MP-40 out of the bow case. He lifted it and pressed the trigger and the machine pistol jumped in his hands. He stitched a line of holes in the ceiling. The brass went on rattling and then tinkling on the worn wooden floor.

People dived for the floor or stayed rooted in the chairs, hands to ears. Someone sobbed. Morgan Taliaferro Martin turned and looked at Du Pré flatly, her eyes as old as Egypt.

Du Pré looked over at Angela Green; she sat with her mouth open and one hand to her face.

"Count them holes, the ceiling," said Du Pré. "Sixteen of 'em, that's how many dead we got here. Fool kids, plain fools, Packy, and Banning. Lot of holes there. You who did this, you are so big, you go to those holes, call those kids out of them. Call Packy. Call the four people killed up in the mountains, just doing their job. Call Corey Banning. Call them out now, I see them, then I go away."

Clark Martin stared at Du Pré, eyes sleepy.

"I have pretty well figured this all out," said Du Pré. "But if I have not, I throw my badge in the ditch, I don't throw my gun, and I come for you. I don't care no more. I don't care, me."

"Mr. Du Pré," said Morgan Martin, "this is appalling. Simply awful. I'll see you prosecuted for this."

Du Pré slid the machine pistol back in the bow case.

"Night that those four were killed, up in the mountains, with the wolves, someone flew up there, in a helicopter," said Du Pré. "But there was this. There were one, maybe two people been flown up there before. Early, before them wolves and biologists were. Waited, in the snow, and then when the helicopter came back, make a lot of noise, them

196

four people all walk toward the helicopter, wondering what it was doing there, and not looking behind them. Probably had maybe a television station's letters stuck on the side."

Du Pré picked up the bow case and he walked to the door and he turned.

"We are ver' close now," he said, "and we come to you, who did this, soon. Until then, though, you remember, there is no more of this. It is enough. Now, you have your damn meeting."

Du Pré walked out, leaving the door open. He stepped across the puddle at the foot of the steps and he opened the back door of Harvey's government car and he slid the bow case on the seat and then he shut the door and opened the front door and he got in.

He slammed the door hard.

"Sometime," said Du Pré, "you lose on that poker, you got to make lucky with them dice."

"Did I hear automatic-weapon fire in there?" said Harvey. "Of course not. Firecrackers. Somebody was celebrating. Firecrackers are illegal, too. Especially as big as those sounded. Terrible, but out of my jurisdiction. Don't suppose you'd like to tell me just what the fuck is going on."

"Kids these days," said Du Pré, "they don't respect nothin'."

Harvey turned the car around and headed back toward Toussaint.

"We can't be late to take Madelaine out for pink wine," said Harvey.

Du Pré rolled a cigarette and he lit it and rolled his window down.

"Yah," said Du Pré, "that is important for sure."

"You think that did any good?" said Harvey.

"Maybe," said Du Pré. "Depends how many people were in on this. I don't think many. We'll see."

They rode in silence for a while.

"Your Madelaine, think she'll dance again with a Blackfeet?" said Harvey.

"Oh, I am sure that she will," said Du Pré.

✤ CHAPTER 37 ✤

You sure she'll come?" said Harvey. He sipped his coffee. They were sitting in the Toussaint Bar. It was about ten in the morning. The place stank of bleach and stale beer and old cigarettes.

Du Pré shrugged.

Shit, I am tired, he thought. I am very tired of this. Also it makes me very sad.

The front door was open and thick shafts of light stabbed through it. Du Pré heard a magpie scrawk.

A truck pulled up outside and stopped. There was a diesel throb for a few minutes, then the engine died and a door slammed.

Angela Green came through the door, the light behind her. She wore a light fringed jacket and a new Stetson. She stood a moment, her eyes adjusting to the dimness. She saw Du Pré and Harvey Wallace sitting at the bar and she walked over. She dragged a stool away from the bar and put it in front of them and she sat down.

"You set them up," said Harvey.

Angela looked at him, her face blank.

"They set themselves up," she said. "All they had to do was stay home and mind their own damn business. Taylor . . . nobody knew he was going to go to war. And that's the story."

"Taylor was a mighty man," said Harvey, "but he was just the one. Took more than that, more than him."

"Taylor was plenty," said Angela. "Now, if you want to talk to me anymore, maybe you should arrest me."

"In time," said Harvey, "though I doubt it. You probably knew what would happen. Probably. But Taylor wouldn't have let you know anything for sure."

"He was always a gentleman," said Angela.

"Yeah," said Harvey, "well, you be a lady and quit spying on those idiot flatlander environmentalists. Leave them to hugging their bunnies in peace. Poor little things'll find some new cause soon anyway. When I do find anything out, though, I will happily arrest you."

Angela lit a cigarette. She looked at Harvey.

"You like this?" she said.

Harvey shrugged.

Susan Klein came out of the kitchen.

"Need something?" she said.

"Ditch," said Angela.

Susan nodded and mixed the drink and pushed it across the bar.

"How're your folks?" she said.

"Thriving," said Angela.

A plastic bag sailed through the door and plopped on the floor. Du Pré and Harvey tensed.

"Look at it," said Clark Martin. He was standing where they couldn't see him. Du Pré got up and he walked over and scooped up the bag, his gun in his right hand. The sun shone on the rutted parking lot, the blacktop, the field beyond the little park.

Du Pré carried the package back to the bar and he set it down and put his gun by it and he pulled it open. Wallets. Four wallets. He opened them. Two had Fish and Wildlife Service badges in them.

"Shit," said Harvey. He had his gun out, too.

199

Angela sipped her drink.

Du Pré looked at Harvey. He nodded.

They went to the doorway. Harvey ducked out in a crouch, pointing his gun.

No one there. Du Pré followed him, walking loose. They went down the steps, squinting in the sun.

Clark Martin was across the road, leaning against one of the box elder trees at the far side of the park, a hundred yards away. He had his arms folded on his chest.

Harvey padded across the road, Du Pré close behind.

"You're under arrest, Clark Martin," said Harvey.

"Stop there," said Clark. Harvey kept on walking.

"It's all there is," said Clark, "me and Taylor. Du Pré was right, Taylor dropped me up there the day before, and when he flew the chopper back they all bunched up. I came in from the trees behind. It was all over in five seconds."

Harvey stopped.

"Get your hands way, way up," he said. He swung up his nine-millimeter. Du Pré came up beside him, gun in hand, not pointing it.

"Show time," said Clark. He jerked his hand into his jacket and pulled out an automatic and he dropped into a crouch and fired.

Du Pré felt something whack him in the chest.

Harvey fired three bursts of two each. Clark Martin shuddered as bullets struck him. He fell back against the tree and tumbled around to the side and fell boneless, like a bundle of rags.

Du Pré felt his chest. It stung where he had been hit. His fingertips felt wax.

Harvey walked on the balls of his feet over to Clark Martin. He kept the gun pointed at him. He kicked Martin's pistol away with his foot and then he knelt and pulled on Martin's shoulder to roll him over. He put his knuckles to Martin's neck. He stood up.

Du Pré came up. He looked down at Clark Martin, his chest red and his eyes glazing.

Harvey scratched at his shirt. He looked at his fingernails.

"Wax," he said.

"Me, too," said Du Pré. "He was pret' quick there."

"Real slugs, I dunno we'd made it," said Harvey. "You didn't fire, did you, Du Pré?"

"No," said Du Pré.

Harvey sighed. He put his gun back in the holster.

"Let's smoke," he said.

Du Pré nodded. He rolled a couple of cigarettes. They stood there, looking down at Clark Martin.

"You figured he'd do this?" said Harvey.

"Yah," said Du Pré. "Them Martins got a lot of Indian in them."

"Could have fooled me," said Harvey. "Makes sense, though."

None of this makes much sense, Du Pré thought. Except that people thought that it did. Little bastards insult this place, everybody who lives here, now they'll be a little scared, maybe. Damn Martins, they took a chance. Didn't work out. Taylor's dead. Clark's dead. When he knew we'd find it out, he come in, make us kill him. Pretty Indian, that.

Bart's Rover roared up, light bar flashing, but no siren.

He drove right into the park, across the scrubby grass. He stopped the car and got out.

"Shit," he said.

"Well," said Harvey Weasel Fat, "it's over."

"Oh?" said Bart.

"I checked the phone records," said Harvey, "and there's nothing there. Angela Green called Montana frequently, but she never called the Martin ranch, not once. Her folks. A couple girlfriends. Taylor gave us a confession.

Clark gave us the evidence. End of story."

"What evidence?" said Bart.

"Four wallets," said Harvey, "two of them from Fish and Wildlife officers."

"Why the hell did he keep those?" said Bart.

"Proof," said Harvey. "We got proof and we got a lot of suppositions. Hardly anyone else in on it, directly, anyway. Other people knew. Sort of. Maybe. When the snow finally melts up there we might find a few things, but only Clark and Taylor were actually there. 'Less someone wants to confess just for the fun of a long prison sentence, this is it, folks, this is all there is."

Bart pulled a yellow rescue blanket out of his Rover. He went to Clark Martin and covered him.

"My superiors are gonna love my report," said Harvey. "As I am the Agent in Charge, I hereby suspend myself pending investigation of this shooting. Thank you, Agent Wallace. Harvey Weasel Fat needs a drink. I'm locking this son-of-a-bitching gun in the trunk. Maybe this time they'll fire me."

Du Pré waited while Harvey shed his belt gear into the trunk of his car. Harvey turned and looked over at the park. Bart was scribbling in a notebook.

They went on into the saloon.

Angela Green was sitting at the bar, and Susan Klein was with her. Both of them were crying.

Du Pré mixed a couple of ditchwater highballs.

They took their drinks to a table in the corner.

"To brave men," said Harvey.

Du Pré nodded.

They drank.

"You know this was going to happen this way?" said Harvey.

Du Pré looked down at his glass.

"Thing about brave men," he said, "is that you can trust them."

✤ CHAPTER 38 ✤

Well," said Madelaine, "you are coming? Yes?"

"No, I am not goddamn coming," said Du Pré.

I got to shout, I'll shout, he thought, I will yell very loud.

"They call me, ask that you come."

Christ.

"I am not going to Clark Martin's funeral," said Du Pré. "I did not go to Taylor's, I will not go to this."

"You are wrong."

Madelaine was dressed in black. She had a little Bible and her rosary on the kitchen table.

A shadow went past the window. Du Pré saw Benetsee's shock of dirty white hair bob twice, and then pass the edge of the window frame. Du Pré threw open the kitchen door.

"You old shit," he said, "now what you want? You are never around when I need to talk to you. What you come here for?"

"Go to funeral with you," said Benetsee. "What you think? Du Pré, you know them Martin people, eh? Taylor, Clark, they are brave. You be brave, too."

"Christ," said Du Pré, "I don't got to have both of you, you know."

"You got both of us, sure enough," said Madelaine. "You go get dressed now, get your fiddle. They were good warriors, now you go play a song for them and the ravens. Huh. I don't think this is a good time to be late.''

Du Pré put on his worn clothes and he walked out to the Rover. Madelaine and Benetsee were already sitting in it. Benetsee grinned and chuckled.

Du Pré got in. He looked down at the console between the front seats. Madelaine had put his fiddle there.

''I am not liking this,'' said Du Pré. ''I sort of helped kill them both, you know.''

''Shut up and drive this or I will,'' said Madelaine.

The day was cold and overcast; it had rained in the early morning. The backs of the cattle in the pastures steamed in the gray light. The sky hung down low and there was no wind at all.

Du Pré drove fast, not speaking. Benetsee and Madelaine chattered about good places to pick morel mushrooms. Asparagus. Logged places where stump mushrooms would grow by the hundredweight.

When Du Pré got to the turnoff that went into the Martin ranch's holdings, he stopped the Rover.

''I don't like this,'' said Du Pré.

Benetsee cracked him hard in the head with the knuckles of his left hand.

''This white world is not good for very much,'' he said. ''Now, you just remember some Indian in you, I hit you till you do. Clark and Taylor are still around, won't leave till maybe next spring. You don't come and honor them, they will be hurt.''

''Shit,'' said Du Pré. He went on down the gravel road. It was four miles in to the main ranch house. The Martins had their own graveyard, a quarter of a mile from the dozen buildings of the old homestead.

There were a couple hundred trucks and cars parked in orderly rows out in a hay meadow that shouldered over next to the creek. A straggling line of couples, families, and groups was moving toward the grove of birches where the graves lay.

"Damn," said Du Pré, "I will not take my fiddle."

"OK," said Benetsee, "I carry it for you."

Du Pré pulled off and parked and got out and walked around and he opened Madelaine's door and helped her down. Benetsee was on his own. Madelaine took his arm and tugged him along toward the birches over by the chuckling water of the little creek.

They stood at the back of the crowd and listened while the minister spoke the simple burial service. Du Pré could see Morgan Taliaferro Martin standing with the wives of Taylor and Clark, and her grandchildren. Nine of them, the biggest two boys over six feet, gangly, with dark blond hair and big hands. Du Pré saw the little girl who had laughed as she danced with her father, his big boots under her tiny feet.

Someone tugged at Du Pré's elbow. He turned his head and there was Angela Green, Benetsee grinning behind her. The old man had lit a huge twist of sweet grass. The pungent smoke swirled softly in the still air.

"You come with me," whispered Angela. "The family wants you to play a song. One for the lost sons of the voyageurs."

Du Pré nodded. Angela led him around the crowd, up by a bower thick with red-purple lilacs. The bees in the flowers buzzed sleepily. Rain was coming.

The minister stopped and Clark Martin's wife came from the family group and she laid a bundle of flowers, iris and lilacs, on the coffin. Then some men in ranch clothes picked up the coffin and lowered it down into the grave.

Du Pré checked his fiddle for tune. Pret' good.

Morgan Martin looked at him. She nodded.

Du Pré played a lament for a young voyageur lost beneath the dark waters, homeward bound to his love. The song spoke of hardship and courage and loss, and then how from this, friends, remembering him, sang to his love when they finally got home.

It was a fairly long piece, and Du Pré let the last note fade and he put his fiddle to his side and he heard a faint sound that grew and grew. It came from the forest over the creek, the drone of the bagpipes, skirling.

The piper played the first movement of "Brave Caledonia," and then rolled gently to a long drone, and then to the sad "Flowers of the Forest."

Plenty sad music, thought Du Pré. Plenty sad time.

Benetsee was behind him. Sweet-grass smoke purled out of the lilac bower.

The Martin family walked slowly away, back toward the ranch house. The crowd didn't move until they had gone up the steps and the door had closed behind them.

"The Piper in the Forest," Du Pré thought. One of my cousins does that song, plays it on the concertina.

Du Pré walked back to Madelaine. She was praying, as always, for everybody.

Du Pré waited until Madelaine lifted her head. Her eyes were bright with tears.

"Ver' nice," she said. "Now you glad you come?"

Du Pré nodded.

"Where is Benetsee?" she said.

Du Pré shrugged.

He looked round for the old man but he had gone, drifting into the dark trees. He would make his own way home.

We all got to.

"OK," said Madelaine. "We go now, the bar, get me some pink wine, maybe dance a little. You quit being so damn sad, Du Pré, everybody they do what they have to. It is over now, I think, yes?"

It is not over, Du Pré thought. A song ends. Music never does.

"Yes," he said. "We go there. I could use maybe a little whiskey."

"You don't have to be a deputy no more," said Madelaine. "Bart, he don't have to be Sheriff."

Bart was behind them a hundred yards or so, talking to Lawyer Foote.

They walked a little faster and got to the Rover before many people had begun to drive out of the hayfield. Du Pré backed up and turned and bumped out on the road. There was a truck up ahead of them, moving fast.

Angela Green.

Well, Du Pré thought, I am going to quit this deputy shit right now. No more. No more of this.

He sped down the county road toward Toussaint, the Rover sometimes going a little soft on the turns as the gravel rolled under the tires. There were no cars in front of the bar when he turned in and parked.

Susan Klein looked up briefly when they walked in, and back down at the book she was reading.

"How was it?" she said, when Du Pré and Madelaine came up to the bar.

"Ver' sad," said Du Pré, "but nice, too. At the end of the service a piper started to play off in the woods."

"That music, it always makes me cry," said Madelaine. "Maybe it is one of those Scots, my great-grandfather in me."

"They dumped some more wolves up there," said Susan Klein. "You'd think the dumb bastards would know when to quit."

"Eh?" said Du Pré.

"In this morning's paper," said Susan. "It's on the table there."

Du Pré looked down at the Billings newspaper's headlines. Some idiot reporter thought dropping wolves by night was just wonderful. So did the editorial writer.

Du Pré sipped his drink.

❧ CHAPTER 39 ❧

Du Pré watched the fire of the welding rod melting, through the thick, dark green visor on his face. He smelled the acrid stink of burning metal and felt the spatter of molten steel on his boots.

He flipped up his heavy face mask and looked at the weld. Good and tight and well filled. He walked two steps to the water barrel and doused it, hissing.

He ground the weld down and then he heated the spring with a torch and doused it several times to temper it.

Looking good. These things they sit here, what, maybe seventy years now and I got to expect that they get a little bad.

"Du Pré!"

Du Pré turned and looked toward the bright light of the doorway. Booger Tom was outlined in it, Benetsee standing behind his right shoulder.

"Ya kin leave off for a moment and come settle an argument," said Booger Tom.

Du Pré set the steel down and he took off the heavy leather welding coat and the mask and he put them on their pegs and he fished around in his shirt pocket for his tobacco and papers and he went outside with the little white bag in his hand.

He rolled a smoke for Benetsee and one for Booger Tom and he lit them and then rolled one for himself.

The July day was close and cloudy and promised hard short rain at sundown. Now, in the afternoon, silver sheets fell from the black clouds but the rain evaporated before it hit the ground. Thunder rumbled. A jet plane drew a white line high past the sinking sun.

Du Pré fished around in his car and found his whiskey and a half-gallon jug of screwtop white he kept there in case he ran into Benetsee.

They walked round back of the old place to the little creek and sat on log seats under the lilac bushes Du Pré had planted years before, when he and Bart had found out the sad story of Du Pré's father and Bart's brother, joined now in death, one made the other and it was all too late but for a good story, maybe.

Bart's Rover pulled in up front and some of Jacqueline's many children ran laughing toward it. He never came without something for them, and he never talked down to the kids.

"Which one a us is the biggest liar," said Booger Tom, "me or ol' Too Many Feathers here?"

Du Pré looked at the two old monsters for a long moment.

"I am just a brand inspector, deputy, fiddler," he said finally, "and that is a question for an astronomer. It is too big, me."

Benetsee laughed and he washed out an old jam jar in the creek and he poured himself wine.

Du Pré and Booger Tom passed the whiskey back and forth.

"Benetsee and me been playing cards," said Booger Tom. "We both cheat pretty good, so we're about even."

"Him, he cheat more," said Benetsee.

"I don't care which, you old shits, cheat more," said Du Pré. "I got things, you know, to think on besides that."

Benetsee cut a willow stem and he began to notch it and

he twisted the red stick in his old hands and the bark spun and he slipped it free. He carved a moment and put the bark back on and fingered the holes he had made. He made a couple bigger and then he began to play, a pipe tune, old Métis song, dance on the buffalo hide pegged to the ground.

Song about people making their meat, in the fall, there, kill them buffalo, cut the meat into sheets, hang it in the sun and fire. Let it dry good, pack it away. Pound it to powder, mix with the dried chokecherry and Indian plums. Heat the marrow fat and pour it some salted over the mixed powdered meat and dried fruit. Eat it when the sun dogs ride the sky and the cold has claws reach through your chest to your heart.

Du Pré got his fiddle, he tuned it a moment, and he played a slow song some voyageur had made up on a moonless night when the lake was smooth and full of stars and the loons called far off, and then he heard the loup-garou, the werewolf, scream in the dark and he knew it smelled his blood and was following. Song prays for protection all things that are evil, when they come they cannot find you.

They heard Bart's booming laugh and the squeals of the happy kids.

Du Pré had a slug of whiskey. He rolled another smoke.

His horses curled back on each other, up to the fence, curious about who was here.

Benetsee played another tune. Du Pré listened, nodding. He finished.

"That for Prairie Falcon Woman," he said.

Poor Corey, Du Pré thought, you did your best.

"Yeah," said Du Pré, "well, it be some quiet now, I think."

Benetsee laughed. He roared with laughter.

"Sure," said Booger Tom, "now maybe you just tell me

which three of them packhorses you want and quit lyin' by not even botherin' to lie to me."

Du Pré laughed.

"OK," he said, "I want them two grullas and the big bay. I am about done with them welding anyway."

A couple of big helicopters whacked and whacked off in the distance, headed up into the Wolfs. Two smaller helicopters followed.

"There they go," said Booger Tom. "Don't learn for shit, do they?"

"I be there, a minute," said Du Pré.

He went into the shed and picked up two of the wolf traps, and he brought them out and set them down and he rolled them up in some canvas. And two more. Two more. Two more.

They weighed fifty pounds apiece, with the long chains on them.

Six wolf traps, all oiled and scraped free of rust.

"I ain't seen any of those since I was wet three places, includin' behind the ears," said Booger Tom.

Du Pré nodded.

Booger Tom and Benetsee walked back to the pasture with catch-ropes and they dropped loops over the necks of the grullas and led them out the swinging wooden gate. The tough little horses came willingly.

Booger Tom and Benetsee tied them to a post and they went to the tack shed and came out with two packsaddles and blankets and ropes and they began to pack the horses.

Madelaine came, parking her old car on the grass by the drive. She lifted saddlebags of food and such out of her trunk and walked back to the men.

Du Pré knelt by the little creek. Brook trout darted in the water's dapple.

Drink this water all my life. Tastes of fish piss. I like it.

Live under them mountain all my life.

See that rain never get to the ground every summer.

See them sun dogs in the cold black winter.

My people they were here, they are here by maybe 1700.

My great-great-grandpa he fight with little Gabriel Dumont, he come down here after the 1886 Rebellion, them Red River people, and he raise his family, pick them mussel shell for the button makers. Never know how to read and write, but he is a great fiddler. His name was Gabriel, too.

Pretty fine country.

Du Pré stood up.

"They drop them wolf off now," said Madelaine. "Got the TV crews up there, you know."

Du Pré nodded.

"Yeah, well, you know, my grandpapa he hunt down that last pair buffalo wolves with that Don Stevens," he said, "long, long time ago."

Them wolves have names.

Old Snowdrift and Lady Snowdrift, almost white wolves, them. Old Snowdrift the biggest wolf ever killed, I hear.

Du Pré went out to the pasture and he whistled and his mountain horse, old Walkin' Tom, came over, whuffling. The horse was getting old but was still sound and Du Pré had ridden him always and if he left without him the horse would grieve. Then he'd just jump the fence and come along anyway.

Du Pré opened the gate and the horse followed him back to the tack shed. Du Pré saddled him. He put the food Madelaine had brought on the grullas, helped pack the old bay with the rest.

He picked up his .270 and lashed it on to the bay's load.

Checked his saddlebags for tobacco and whiskey.

They loaded the horses into Bart's huge trailer and then

Bart pulled it up to his ranch and on up the access road that led to the trail to the Wolfs, the quickest route to the pass above.

They offloaded the stock and checked the knots and Du Pré swung up and he took the rope from Booger Tom's hand. He leaned down to kiss Madelaine.

Bart stood there, still the Sheriff.

One of the big helicopters lifted off the top of the mountains, then the other. The little white ones were circling round the place they'd come up from.

"OK," said Du Pré. "Well," he said, touching his hat with his hand, "I thank you. You know, this is my land here. And I like them wolf all right. And when I am ready, they can come back."

He chirred to old Tom and the string followed along.

I got to write a song about this, he thought.